JET SET NURSE

JET SET NURSE

Jane Converse

CHIVERS
THORNDIKE

This Large Print edition is published by BBC Audiobooks Ltd, Bath, England and by Thorndike Press®, Waterville, Maine, USA.

Published in 2004 in the U.K. by arrangement with Maureen Moran Agency.

Published in 2004 in the U.S. by arrangement with Maureen Moran Agency.

U.K. Hardcover ISBN 0–7540–6967–2 (Chivers Large Print)
U.K. Softcover ISBN 0–7540–6968–0 (Camden Large Print)
U.S. Softcover ISBN 0–7862–6596–5 (Nightingale)

The text of this Large Print edition is unabridged.
Other aspects of the book may vary from the original edition.

Set in 16 pt. New Times Roman.

Printed in Great Britain on acid-free paper.

British Library Cataloguing in Publication Data available

Library of Congress Control Number: 2004103122

ONE

During the three months that I had been Durwood Kingsley's private nurse, we had argued almost incessantly. Not angry, hostile arguments; most of our conversations were punctuated with mild laughter, for Durwood had a wry sense of humor and I was badly in need of a change from tears.

But in spite of the light-hearted manner in which my patient and I filled my on-duty hours in his Manhattan penthouse apartment, we were both quite serious about our opposing views.

Our lesser arguments revolved around Durwood's desire to get back to his brokerage office and the exciting atmosphere of the Stock Exchange; there I had doctor's orders to back me up. I had more trouble convincing my handsome patient that I was not the girl he should marry.

He was resting on the chaise longue in his study late one afternoon in January, behind him the vast double plate-glass window which offered a panoramic view of the New York skyline. Forty-five stories below, a chilling wind whipped the city's streets; here, in the elegantly appointed room, with its mahogany paneled walls and thick wine-hued carpeting, a cheerful blaze crackled in the fireplace and a subdued string quartet added to the coziness of the scene, courtesy of an elaborate stereo system that had probably cost more than I earn in a year. Durwood swirled the vegetable juice I had just poured for him in a crystal cocktail glass, sipped at it cautiously, and scowled, 'Perhaps you're right, Roxy. I shouldn't even consider ending my blessed bachelorhood with a girl who can't mix a decent martini.'

I stood over him like a stern mother. 'Drink up. Carrot, tomato and celery juice. Vitamins. Down the hatch.'

He obeyed reluctantly, feigned a shudder and placed the empty glass on an ebony table at his side. 'Serving wholesome drinks in a cocktail glass is supposed to deceive me into thinking I'm enjoying life?'

'Dr. Britton seemed to think you wouldn't know how to hold any other kind of glass,' I said. 'You want to get well, don't you?'

'I'm perfectly well. Just sick of being cooped up in this aerie, having you treat me like a geriatrics case.' There was no genuine resentment in Durwood's tone; this was the sort of banter we kept up during all his waking hours. 'Is that why I'm being rejected, Miss Ferris? Because you've decided I'm old and infirm?'

'Thirty-six isn't old and one heart attack doesn't mean you're infirm,' I said in my most professional manner. 'That is, providing you take care of yourself. Now that you've stopped smoking and drinking . . .'

'And earning a living, you might add.'

I laughed and perched myself on the arm of a leather chair. ' "Earning a living"! Honestly, to hear you talk, a person would think you'll have to apply for relief if you don't get back to that idiotic Stock Exchange tomorrow morning. Two or three more weeks of rest. Just two or three more weeks, and then you won't have me telling you what to do. You can plunge right back into all that . . . pressure and hectic insanity that gave you a coronary in the first place.'

'*Good!*' Durwood grinned, his fingers running along the satin lapels of his black smoking jacket. It was a nervous habit he had developed since he had been forced to give up cigarettes. 'Excellent. I can't wait.'

I shook my head back and forth slowly. 'You're hopeless, Mr. Kingsley. But *why?* Why would you want to . . .'

'Because it's my idea of fun. Some men gamble on horses, I gamble on products. It's a game. I enjoy it.'

As always, he was pleasant in his explanation. I couldn't imagine Durwood showing annoyance, let alone anger. Urbane, poised, he was a product of upper-class breeding and education without being a snob. He had sharply defined, sensitive features, mahogany-colored hair meticulously groomed to take advantage of natural waves, and sideburns tinged with just enough gray to lend him a distinguished air. Durwood's eyes, rimmed with dark lashes that I envied, were of a uniquely attractive apple green shade, and they viewed the world with a calm knowingness that was free of cynicism.

Tall, handsome, charming company and considered a financial genius at the age of thirty-six, Durwood Kingsley III headed the eligible bachelor list of many a socialite hostess, yet he had actually proposed marriage to *me*. It was hard to explain to my friends why I had turned my back on a future with this man who repeatedly let it be known that he 'adored' me. Certainly it wasn't easy to explain it to Durwood himself.

Let it be known to all and sundry that while I fall into the petite gamine category that some men find appealing, I am eons removed from being a ravishing beauty. My mouth is too big, both literally and figuratively. Too big for my turned-up nose, anyway. And the nose happens to be liberally sprinkled with freckles. A chic hairdresser eyeing my ash blond hair would probably shriek at the careless cut; I wear it short, comb it, let the crazy curls fall where they want to fall, and hope for the best. I suppose oversized blue eyes are supposed to be an asset; Bill Hardin used to rave about my eyes. But looking into a mirror I always see this hopelessly unsophisticated urchin with a

4

look of perpetual astonishment on her face.

As for comparing my family background with that of Durwood . . . well, forget it. My mother died when I was twelve and Pop raised seven of us kids by riding up and down an elevator all day in an uptown office building. Part of my salary goes to keep my two youngest brothers from becoming juvenile delinquents by seeing that they stay in high school and have shoes to wear when they go. If it hadn't been for that scholarship, I wouldn't have gotten through nurses' training.

So here I was, getting over a traumatic experience with a medical student who had suddenly decided (after I'd paid the printer for our wedding invitations) that he (a) didn't want to be a doctor, after all; (b) didn't want to be a married doctor; and (c) wanted to go to San Francisco, study Zen Buddhism, write poetry and learn to play the sitar. Nice. I can make funnies about it now, being a Pagliacci type. When you have a turned-up nose and freckles, you *have* to be funny; none of this sitting back and just being beautiful for the likes of me. So, being a clown on the surface, I can say, 'Bill Hardin traded me for an East Indian banjo' and grin about it. But at the time, I'd have taken first prize in any soggy pillow contest. From seven until three I did general duty at the hospital; the rest of the time I bawled.

Durwood Kingsley, with his mature,

understanding attitude, was a natural wailing wall for me. Recovering from his heart attack in the hospital, he became a combination father confessor and sympathetic buddy, and, of course, I told him about my miserable experience. By the time Durwood was ready to continue his convalescence in that plush apartment of his, it seemed only natural to accept the invitation to work as his private nurse.

He had given me sensible, paternal advice: 'Get busy and forget this immature character. If he's that unstable, you're lucky you didn't get stuck with him for life.' Now, after several months of the most relaxing relationship I had ever known, Durwood was hardly being sensible (why risk another coronary when he already had more than enough money to live the good life?), and, although he was a gentleman with a capital G, he was no longer thinking of me in paternal terms.

For instance, that afternoon, as he finished telling me why he refused to give up his brokerage business, Durwood faced me with a quizzical stare and asked, 'Is that why I can't talk you into joining the Kingsley clan? Because you're afraid I'll be clipping coupons on our honeymoon?'

I was supposed to be amused, but Durwood had come too close to the truth for comfort. 'That's carrying the idea to extremes, but . . . well, look. Your whole life is built around something I can't even begin to understand. Bulls and bears and futures and . . . don't you see, I couldn't care less about stocks and bonds. I couldn't marry someone who . . .'

'Bores you to tears? I haven't done that, have I, Roxy?' Durwood appeared hurt.

'No, no, it's just that . . .' I searched for a painless way to tell him that I'm a romantic idealist. Since the day I decided that I wanted to be an R.N., I hadn't been able to visualize marrying any man who didn't share my interest in medicine. I may sound like a lightweight, but when it comes to helping sick people, especially little kids, I'm dead serious. So that meant telling Durwood that I couldn't marry him because he wasn't a doctor, which would have sounded ridiculous. Especially since I'd just been jilted by a would-be medic.

I decided to use the equally honest, but more logical excuse: 'Durwood, I like you. I've never had more respect for any person, and it's a cinch no one's ever been kinder, more considerate . . .'

'But you don't love me.'

I avoided those penetrating green eyes. 'I know what you're going to say. I should have learned my lesson about the kind of love where bells ring and the whole world's one great big valentine. I'm cured of that little episode, thanks to you. I think I could see Bill Hardin walk into this room right now and . . . nothing would happen. But marrying someone

7

. . . unless you have a lot in common and you're . . . very much in love . . .' I looked over to see Durwood eyeing me with a melancholy expression. 'All right, let's just say our life styles are too different. Here you are, with all the money you're ever going to need, ready to go back and kill yourself making more. If I were in your position . . .'

I had paused, not quite sure of what I'd do in Durwood's circumstances. He urged me on, his voice soft and, it seemed to me, somewhat wistful: 'What would you do, Roxy?'

'Well, I'd . . . start enjoying life, for one thing. I'd travel. I'd see something of the world. I don't know. Maybe that wouldn't appeal to you, so who am I to give advice?' I got to my feet abruptly, picked up the tray next to Durwood's chaise longue, and started for the kitchen. This was not the first time I had tried to escape the uncomfortable subject.

I was almost out of the room when Durwood said, 'Don't run off. Suppose I met you halfway, Roxy? Would you be willing to stay with me? See the emergence of the new Durwood Kingsley?'

I turned, puzzled by Durwood's not wholly facetious tone. 'Stay with you as your nurse? You aren't going to need a nurse if you take care of yourself. Relax a little.'

'That's what I'm proposing.' Durwood waved at a footstool near his longue. 'Sit down a minute and let me tell you what I have in mind.' When I had settled myself again, he went on. 'You aren't the only person who's been pressuring me to get away from my business. I had another call from my cousin Marlaine last night.'

'Oh—the *really* rich member of the family,' I remembered. 'Yes, you told me something about her.'

Durwood smiled. 'Right. Much-married Marlaine. She's made up for my single state. I've lost count now, but I think her new husband is number five.'

I made a disparaging motion with my head. 'I wasn't recommending *that* sort of change for you.'

'I'm sure you weren't. Point is, Marlaine isn't simply concerned with getting me to join her on this Caribbean island-hopping vacation she's lined up. I think she's more interested in you.'

'She's never even met me!' I protested.

'I've told her about you. And she needs a . . . sort of nurse-companion for my niece.' Durwood adjusted himself to a more comfortable position. 'Let me paint the picture for you. My cousin didn't have to be clever to get *her* money. Her mother left Marlaine a sizable fortune, though I suspect she's gone through most of it by now. She's part of the jet set, and all the expenses that entails. I can't say that I've approved, Marlaine keeping her teenaged daughter in expensive boarding schools while she zipped around the globe, throwing away money and collecting husbands.'

Marlaine Whatever-Her-New-Name-Was sounded like someone I wasn't anxious to meet, and I'm sure Durwood guessed my thoughts because he said, 'She's a mixed-up character, but surprisingly likable. And if she behaves herself, she's in line to inherit the Kingsley Paper Mill fortune.' A vague smile crossed Durwood's face. 'Her father . . . my uncle Ben Kingsley . . . revolutionized the sandwich bag, among other things.'

'If she "behaves herself"?' I repeated. 'What does that mean?'

'It means that my uncle's an extreme puritan. Old Ben's been threatening to cut Marlaine out of his will . . . leave that big bundle to some fundamentalist church if his daughter doesn't give up what he calls her "wild and sinful ways." Frankly, Marlaine's worried. She's either got to settle down with her new husband and make a home for Gee Gee . . . that's my niece . . . or she's going to have to adjust to buying ready-made dresses off the rack.'

'Then what's this island-hopping expedition you were talking about?' I asked. 'That doesn't sound like "settling down" to me.'

'Well, the way Marlaine explains it, she has the other problem of getting Gee Gee adjusted to her new stepfather.' Durwood sighed. 'Personally, I think this is going to be

10

one last glorious fling before Marlaine goes through the motions of being a proper wife and mother. My presence in the party might add a note of respectability.' With a slight hint of embarrassment at what sounded like immodesty, Durwood explained, 'My uncle respects anyone who's amassed money without help from him. And then there's Marlaine's interest in you. Without even knowing about this safari of hers, I gave you quite a build-up.'

I grinned. 'I suppose you told her I was an exceptionally wholesome character.'

Durwood returned the grin. 'As a matter of fact, I did. And Marlaine thinks you'd be an ideal addition to her party. Good influence on Gee Gee. Who, not incidentally, suffers from some sort of nervous or . . . emotional problem.'

After four stepfathers and a mother who dumped her off in a series of spiffy boarding schools, that didn't sound too surprising, but I spared Durwood my opinion of his relatives. He didn't want to talk about Gee-Gee or Marlaine, anyway; my patient was only paving the way for more personal interests. He had been speaking casually, indicating no deep interest in the comings and goings of his wealthy cousin: Now he leveled a somber stare in my direction, his voice assuming a correspondingly serious pitch. 'I'd like to go, Roxy. Partly because you're right . . . I could stand a little change of pace. But mostly to give you a chance to see me as something other than a . . . a bedridden old goat with a tickertape where his mind ought to be.'

I started to protest, 'But I've never thought . . .'

Durwood waved away my protest. 'You couldn't help thinking I'm dull. Now you have an opportunity to do the very things you've said you would do if you were financially well off. Travel. Meet new people, see new places. Marlaine loves to surround herself with people. She thinks nothing of flying to Rome for a brunch with friends and jetting to Paris for a cocktail party at five. It sounds exhausting to me, but I have Marlaine's word that it's . . . what were her words? . . . "madly divine kicks".'

I couldn't even guess, at the time, whether Durwood or his cousin were right. All I knew was that a pleasantly persuasive man was urging me to join a fun venture that, until then, I wouldn't have entertained even in my daydreams. He was talking about moonlit nights on a Caribbean cruiser, glistening white sand beaches, stewards carrying cooling drinks and gourmet dinners to me at the side of a sun warmed azure blue swimming pool. I made a hasty comparison with me carrying trays to the bedside of some dour old dyspeptic patient (painting the worst possibility, so that a sudden surge of dedication would not change my mind and deprive me of this once-in-a-lifetime opportunity) and, after that, my decision was obvious. 'When do we leave?' I asked.

Durwood virtually glowed his delight. 'Marlaine's rather impetuous. You'll need an advance and time to shop for a vacation wardrobe.' He blew me a playful kiss. 'Would six days do it? We're flying to Trinidad a week from today.'

TWO

On the chartered jet, zooming toward Trinidad, I had my first opportunity to wonder if my travel urge should have been satisfied by a budget tour of Yellowstone Park, paid for out of my own meager savings.

Marlaine Hayden (for that was her new name) had gathered around her an entourage of motley characters, most of whom I would have avoided in the subway. As a matter of fact, apart from Durwood, who kept beaming at me and gauging my reaction to this sudden deluge of glamour, there were only two people in the party of twelve who appealed to me at all, and I've never been known for my selectivity. (Falling in love with Bill Hardin was a case in point!)

Let me try to recall, first, the people I could have done without. Wesley Reed probably rates being at the head of the list. A dapper, dark-haired bachelor of about thirty, he had heavy-lidded black eyes that seemed to be forever assaying what he could get out of whom. Among his affectations were a wispy, pencil-line moustache, a ridiculously long gold cigarette holder, a paisley silk ascot tie that probably cost as much as my entire wardrobe, and a pseudo-sexy manner that made my skin crawl. From what I could gather from the conversations on the plane, Wesley was a professional ladies' man. Durwood told me that Mr. Reed had developed his taste for expensive clothing, cars, vacations and vintage wines while serving as social secretary for a wealthy dowager, now deceased. Apparently the old girl had not left Wesley enough money to indulge his tastes, but a sufficient amount to go on the prowl for a new benefactress, preferably one he could rope into marriage. I know that he lost interest in me the instant he learned I was a mere working girl. Amazingly, considering that Marlaine had just acquired a new husband, Wesley Reed seemed to be concentrating his attention on the paper heiress.

Then there was Irena Travalgnini, Marlaine's personal astrologer, numerologist, all-around 'psychic adviser' and confidante. She was introduced to me as 'The Countess Irena,' but no one specified the country in which she did her countessing. A towering, heavy-set Amazon of a woman, she wore her long lavender-tinted white hair pulled back from a turtle-like face and neck and tied back in a pony tail. The hairdo would have suited a female thirty years her junior, for Irena was easily in her fifties. A deep tan had parched her coarse, heavily painted features, and there was no square inch of the Countess' earlobes, fingers or neck that didn't drip with massive, ornate jewelry. Another ring on her parched hands would have tilted her to starboard. Feigning a mystic air, Irena Travalgnini evidently kept her place in this fast-moving company by playing on the credulity of its bored members.

There were other equally deep tans, belonging to a scattering of younger people who seemed to know a great deal about tennis, racing cars and horses, but not much else. Oldest of the lot was Marlaine's 'dear, dear friend' Tish Vandercourt, recently divorced from a Texas oilman and currently being squired by a muscle-bound health fiend named Bunny Stafford IV. I don't know what the previous three Bunnies did to pass their time; this one flexed his biceps, flashed toothpaste-ad teeth and kept his somewhat dissipated and older dream girl supplied with martinis. Everyone seemed to assume that I knew of Bunny's fantastic successes on the tennis court, and regarded me as a cretin when they learned I didn't.

They also took it for granted that I had seen

all of Yvette Girardoux's French 'art films,' though I had never before heard of that petite minx-like creature. From my brief experience with narcotics addicts at the clinic in New York, I guessed that Yvette shunned liquor because she had found a more potent escape from reality. It was just a hunch, but her glassy eyes were only one of the symptoms I recognized.

I was sadly uneducated, too, in not recognizing pot-bellied, fortyish Prince Alexei Pribiloff as one of the true heirs to the Russian throne. (Being restored to the monarchy was a very likely possiblity, if thrones can be regained by playing bridge and drinking Scotch on the rocks.) I was even lax in knowing that the Colombian aristocrat who looked like a grossly exaggerated Xavier Cugat was, indeed, *the* Ernesto Sandoval de Lopez de Sevilla. Very impressive if you're passionately interested in *fincas*. A finca, I deduced, was a coffee plantation. Ernesto had more fincas than most of us have trading stamps.

There were others, most of whom, happily, don't come to mind at the moment. But, as I said earlier, the only two who struck me as something other than characters out of one of those old Grade-B movies you see on television if you're foolish enough to stay up all night being assailed by used car commercials, were Marlaine and Noah Hayden.

I'll start with Noah, because I liked him more than I had any business liking a man who had just recently married my new employer. I would have sworn, at Kennedy Airport, that the rangy, quiet man with the thoughtful blue eyes (almost *sad* eyes, I thought) was introduced to me as *Dr.* Hayden. Nothing more was said during the flight about what kind of doctor he was, or had been. Maybe a veterinarian, for all I knew; the horsey jet set seem to venerate their vets along with their analysts.

Anyway, Noah's handsome face and serious manner rang immediate bells with me. Even his smile, which was slow and rare, brought out some sort of maternal instinct in me. On second thought, maternal isn't exactly the word; Noah Hayden looked as out of place in this crowd as I did, and I had a crazy yen to put my arms around him, assuring him that there were still a few people around who didn't gush, 'Darling, how absolutely *mad!*' with every other sentence.

But, then, Noah wasn't exactly a little boy lost in the woods. He was married to one of the most striking and outgoing women I had ever met.

Durwood's cousin was easily the cog around which this purposeless social wheel revolved. If you looked at her too closely, or watched her movements, you were aware of the fatigue lines imprinted on her slender face by her jet-

17

paced mode of existence. You noticed the trembling of her long pale fingers as her hands waved around in animated gestures, hands, incidentally, that were always snuffing out a cigarette or holding up a fresh one for some obliging male's lighter. Her nervous laughter (and Marlaine laughed a lot) was another dead giveaway; under the carefree, madcap exterior, Marlaine was a coiled tension spring. I learned later that my first instinct about her had been correct; the tinny laughter, the endless jokes and zany ideas were a cover-up for Marlaine's desperate unhappiness with the mess she had made of her life.

Still, I found her warmth sincere. She wanted to be liked by everyone, and Marlaine worked at it with a manic energy. Oh, and did I mention that she was stunningly beautiful? Her flaming red hair, which would probably have reached to her waist if combed down, was piled high in an elaborate coiffure that made her look extremely tall, though she was no taller than I. Like most naturally red-haired people, she had a pale complexion which couldn't take the sun. Her fine skin contrasted like ivory with the bronzed faces of her friends. Marlaine's eyes, like Durwood's, were of that uniquely attractive green that was apparently a hallmark of the Kingsley clan.

Too thin. That was my first impression. Marlaine Hayden had the scrawny build of one of those emaciated models who pose for high-

18

fashion magazines. As a nurse, I would have recommended three wholesome meals daily and a minimum of eight hours' sleep each night; from what I was able to observe, my hostess took her nutrition in liquid form, over the gentle protests of her husband, and sleep, to Marlaine, was a waste of party time.

Not a wholesomely healthy type, then, but in the emerald-green velvet jump suit she had selected for the flight, Marlaine would have commanded attention anywhere. And when she had seen to it that her guests were comfortable on board the chartered plane ('comfortable' meaning that they knew where to replenish their drinks) Marlaine shooed her cousin out of the double seat he had been sharing with me and plunked herself down, the contents of her martini glass sloshing over a little in the process.

She laughed that tinkly who cares? laugh that I had already learned was typical of her, and thanked me for blotting the trousers of that exquisitely cut emerald-green outfit with a handkerchief. 'Don't worry about it, darling. It's an old rag I picked up at the Goodwill. A little booze gives velvet a sort of patina, you know?'

I visualized the price of that 'old rag,' wondering how many sandwich bags Marlaine's father had to sell to pay for it.

Marlaine had already forgotten the incident. Green eyes widening, she apologized because I didn't have a drink. 'What *barbarians* we are! Oh, Roxy, you mean no one's offered to fix your favorite poison?'

'Durwood did,' I assured her. 'It's a little early for me.' It would have startled Marlaine to learn that I didn't care for cocktails at any hour, and certainly not for breakfast.

She smiled, patting my hand. 'You'll learn, baby. It's never too early.' For a flashing moment, a wistful expression clouded those lovely green eyes, and she muttered, 'Usually, it's too late.' She didn't take time to explain that obviously double-edged remark, smiling again and saying, 'If you're being circumspect because you're thinking of yourself as an employee, please forget it, Roxy. I told Durwood I needed someone to look after Gee Gee, but she's not joining us for another week. Some messy complication to straighten out at school, and then I'll have her fly up to meet us.'

I remembered that Gee Gee was supposed to be suffering from a 'nervous ailment,' and I reminded Marlaine that I was a nurse, not a governess or hired companion.

'Oh, Gee Gee needs a nurse,' I was assured. 'She has . . . very definite problems. I expect you'll want to see her medical history. And Noah will want to look into the case, I imagine. He used to be a doctor, you know. An M.D.'

'*Used* to be?' I had a hasty vision of Noah

Hayden being dragged through a malpractice suit, losing his license to practice. 'Isn't he . . . doesn't he . . .'

Marlaine waved her cigarette hand. 'I suppose that once you're an M.D., you're one for life. Sort of like being typed, isn't it? What I mean is that my husband isn't doing any doctoring at the moment. Heaven knows why he'd want to go back to that gruesome grind when he doesn't have to. So many fun things to do. But people get conditioned to drudgery, I suppose. This trip ought to cure him.' Marlaine paused. 'I hope it knits us together as one big happy family. You and Durwood will be loads of help, getting Gee Gee to accept her new stepfather. Poor darling's never really had a sense of . . . you know . . . stability. I suppose you'd say I've been a dreadful excuse for a mother.'

I didn't want to express an opinion, and, fortunately, Marlaine didn't want to hear one. Blithely, as though she were discussing the trivia that made up other conversations around us, Marlaine said, 'I'm sure Gee Gee's a dear. We simply haven't had a chance to get acquainted. And she's never met Noah. I introduced them by telephone and I'm afraid I caught the child in one of her less appealing moods.'

Marlaine went on, chattering brightly, telling me that her husband wanted to establish a permanent residence in California,

21

resume his medical practice, and provide a solid home base for Gee Gee. 'I may be forced into it,' she concluded with a mock sigh. 'What with the pressure from my father, from Noah . . . even from conservative ole Cousin Durwood. Can't you see me showing my begonias to the garden club ladies in some insufferable suburb?' The shudder that accompanied that question was genuine. Then she brightened again. 'It may happen. So, meanwhile, if this is my swan song, it's going to be a dilly. We're going to have a lovely, *love-a-lly* time, darling, and I just wanted you to know that I can't bear being made to feel like a slavedriver. I want you to have scads of fun. Dear . . . are you *sure* we can't get you one little drinkie?'

I was sure. In fact, seeing the sorrowful expression in Noah Hayden's eyes as he came up the aisle a few seconds later, gently but firmly taking the cocktail glass from his wife's hand and suggesting it was time for black coffee, I was more than certain. For all her money, her beauty, her exuberance, her wit, for all her good fortune, not the least of which was being married to a man who made envy logical, I wouldn't have traded places with her. I had made a painful mistake, but I had survived it and learned from it; Marlaine's life was a continuing series of mistakes, and her present course indicated she was headed for more of the same. It seemed a pity, but, then, who was I to tell a full-grown millionairess how to run her life?

I would have been less casual about that observation if I had known how Marlaine's personal nightmare would soon involve me. But I didn't know. And I hadn't been introduced to Gee Gee.

THREE

I had a full week's reprieve before Genevieve (Gee Gee) Sargent, offspring of Marlaine's first marriage, came upon the scene. Slithered is a better word; Gee Gee's every move was reptilian. That first week, most of it spent in a fantastic villa owned by one of Marlaine's innumerable rich friends, blurs in my memory.

I remember a lush tropical setting studded with lush houseguests, each of them changing clothes at least five times daily, racing off to play tennis, raving about the steel band at some newly discovered night spot, finding absurd reasons for staging another party.

Durwood's recent heart attack gave him an excuse whenever the pace got too hectic; he would retire to his room, overlooking that incredibly blue sea and palm lined beach, or he would occupy himself with business correspondence in one of the charming patios, smiling like an indulgent old grandfather at the antics of the younger set. I wasn't seeing Durwood Kingsley in a new light; he was still the conservative, set-in-his-ways bachelor, his body in sun-drenched Trinidad, his heart and mind on Wall Street.

There was some resistance to Marlaine's impetuous ideas from Noah Hayden, too, but usually when his wife would announce, 'Darlings, we're off to St. Kitts. Ginger and Teddy's second anniversary . . . *imagine* those two sticking it out two whole *years!*'—or when Marlaine had a sudden urge to rush off to some remote beach for a lobster and champagne picnic, Noah tagged along indulgently, though with lessening enthusiasm.

Once, during that initial week of island hopping, I got a clue to how completely Noah Hayden was a misfit in this crowd. I remember coming back to the villa after a round of shopping with Marlaine and Irena. On the advice of her 'psychic adviser,' Marlaine had insisted upon buying a raft of chic resort clothes for me in one of those exclusive little shops that cater to well-heeled tourists. I had tried to object, but whenever Irena Travalgnini told Marlaine that the stars or the numbers or the vibrations were 'propitious' for doing something extravagant, Marlaine plunged and there was no arguing with her.

Anyway, we had returned to find all of Marlaine's traveling companions, plus a group of ten or twelve dissolute jet set duplicates who were staying at a plush hotel nearby, lounging around the villa's movie set living room, in varying stages of inebriation and boredom. Now, inactivity, to Marlaine, was like a vacuum that had to be filled instantly. Amazingly, since she had said nothing about the invitation earlier, the flame-haired heiress sang out, 'Darlings . . . you aren't *ready!*' Her tone was mildly admonishing.

Everyone looked up over their rum drinks, eager and hopeful; they were supposed to be ready for something. Something was about to interrupt their deadly ennui. Wonderful, wonderful! Trust Marlaine to keep the action going!

'Lucy Bradshaw's throwing this absolutely *mad* bash at that divine place she's leased over at Charlotte Amalie.'

Wesley Reed, reeking of an expensive cologne that is supposed to make the male animal irresistible, made a game of throwing his arms around Marlaine. 'Lucy's one of my favorite people. How simply superb!' Our dapper gigolo's weary exuberance faded in the next breath. In a world-weary voice, he added, 'Though, confidentially, I can't *bear* that gauche creature she married last. Bruno Something, wasn't it?'

Mention of *any* name invariably created a buzz of malicious gossip. 'Bruno Something' must have been exceedingly unpopular with the group, for there was a boozy

25

cheering response when Marlaine announced, 'Darlings, where have you been? The party is to celebrate Lucy's getting her final decree. Bruno-baby has been *bounced*.'

During the laughter that followed, I noticed that Noah Hayden had come into the room through one of the sliding glass doors that opened onto a patio. No one paid any attention to him as he crossed the room, brushing past Wesley Reed the way a mastiff might walk past a terrier. Noah was stationed next to his wife, and Marlaine had linked her arm through his, when she completed her announcement:

'Now, listen carefully, tigers. We'll fly in exactly three hours, so you'll have to rush to get up your costumes. Lucy wants us to dress as the character we'd most like to be getting divorced from. Isn't that wild?'

There were squeals of delight at Lucy's cleverness, and then Noah's voice, thick with disgust, cut in: 'I think it's the most revolting idea I've ever heard.'

Marlaine looked at her husband with a wounded expression. 'Sweetness, it's only fun!'

A hostile silence had gripped the room; like Bruno Something, Noah had not endeared himself to the jet set. Grim, his face looking as though it had been chipped from granite, Noah said, 'I happen to think that divorce is a tragedy, no matter how it's justified.'

'But, dearest, Bruno was an utter beast,'

Marlaine protested. 'You can't imagine how poor Lucy's suffered. Besides, she's invited him, just to show what a sweet, forgiving soul she is. Lucy is . . .'

'I don't give a damn about Lucy! *Or* Bruno, or their sick idea of a celebration!' Noah's roar was emphasized by a crash of glass as his arm swung out, hurling to the tiled floor a martini pitcher someone had rushed to place before Marlaine moments after she entered the room.

Marlaine's chin quivered, but the embarrassing scene was one she was determined to handle. Lightly, reaching up to pinch Noah's cheek, she said, 'Don't be a spoilsport, love. You'll begin to sound like my fuddy-duddy daddy. We'll all have a perfectly smashing time, and you'll *adore* Lucy. Well stay just for . . .'

'I'm not going,' Noah said quietly. He ignored the baleful stares of Marlaine's friends, paused long enough to look deeply into his wife's eyes, and then added, 'Neither are you.'

He came within inches of me without, I'm sure, being aware of my presence, as he strode out of the room.

Marlaine, I noticed, had tears in her eyes. Any attempt to conceal her misery behind the usual let-us-be-gay facade would have been a dismal failure. She settled for sighing, 'Poor Noah. Maybe the pace is getting him down.'

Irena Travalgnini resolved the problem by

27

croaking, 'I told you, Marlaine. Avoid domestic difficulty. Use the coming four days to shop and catch up with material matters. Your most advantageous social period begins on the twenty-third of this month.'

Irena offered no astrological advice to the others, and though they insisted that the 'divorce party' would be a disaster without Marlaine, the consensus seemed to be that they would go to Lucy's party nevertheless.

Most grief-stricken over this turn of events was Wesley Reed. Just before I escaped the room, I heard that unctuous dandy 'consoling' his hostess, 'Pet, I can understand wifely devotion, but it tears me up inside to see you becoming a virtual lackey. You deserve every second of joy that comes into your life, Marlaine. You're so selfless, and you've gone through such agony. I only wish I could give my life to making you happy, dearest.'

Marlaine was so hungry for approval, *everyone's* approval, everyone's love, that Wesley's pitch was probably not wasted on her. Nevertheless, she followed Noah to their room shortly afterward, for I heard his deep, quiet voice talking to her. His words were unintelligible through the doors that separated us, but I knew that Noah was talking sense to Marlaine, pleading with her to stop drinking, to stop running, to end her shallow existence and begin living as the wife of a dependable, devoted physician.

She must have loved Noah Hayden; at least to the degree that Marlaine was able to love anyone without ever having learned to love and respect herself first. I know that she promised, repeatedly, to 'settle down.' She remembered, too, that her daughter would be arriving the next day; how much cozier it would be for Gee Gee to arrive with her Mommy and her new stepfather 'at home,' and all of the non-family people out of the house. Noah had won that round. Three hours later, apart from an army of servants, there was no one in that magnificent villa by the sea but Durwood Kingsley, the Haydens, and a nurse who was beginning to wonder why she was there.

*   *   *

Gee Gee Sargent arrived two days later while Durwood and I were taking a peaceful stroll along the beach. The Haydens had gone to the airport to meet Marlaine's daughter, and when I returned to the villa they were having a martiniless luncheon on the terrace. Durwood had gone directly to his room to rest; did I want to 'dash upstairs' and introduce myself to Gee Gee? Marlaine, after only two forced days on the wagon, looked radiant. 'The poor child's exhausted, so I scooted her up to your room. There goes your privacy, Roxy. Go up and say hello. You won't find Gee Gee boring,

I'm sure. She's amazingly adult for her tender years.'

Noah's eyes met mine for an instant. 'That,' he said solemnly, 'is the understatement of the atomic age.'

Marlaine's tinkling laughter followed me up the stairs. She was feeling rested, her child was safely at home, her husband was being wonderfully attentive. Looking back now, I think it was the only time I ever saw Marlaine looking genuinely happy.

I don't know what instinct prompted me to enter that luxuriously furnished room, which I had enjoyed in complete privacy until then, with a feeling of trepidation. I had met and cared for all kinds of people; certainly a meeting with a neglected teen-ager shouldn't have shaken me. Minutes later, I was willing to admit that I had never before met anyone as unsettling as Genevieve Sargent. Nor, if I was lucky, would I ever meet anyone like her again.

I found Marlaine's daughter sprawled on one of the twin beds in the room I was to share with her. Her head propped by her arm, she was scribbling into what appeared to be a diary. Her back was turned to me as I closed the door behind myself. She took no notice of my entrance, though she had certainly heard the door. Her small body, strangely voluptuous for a girl just turned sixteen, was clad in brief beige shorts topped by a tangerine silk halter. Her bare toes wriggled nervously in time with the furious scrawling of her hand.

I gave her the benefit of the doubt; perhaps Gee Gee was too absorbed to have heard the door open and close. 'Hello,' I greeted. 'Welcome home, Gee Gee. I'm Roxy Ferris.'

She made no effort to face me. 'I'm singularly unimpressed.' The words were not spoken, they were hissed.

I don't know whether I was more embarrassed or infuriated. I like youngsters; I wasn't so long out of my teens that I couldn't empathize with a sixteen-year-old. But I was far from prepared for this insolent little snip.

I think I would have walked out of Gee Gee's life then and there if she hadn't flopped over, snapping the diary shut as she turned to inspect me. And an inspection it was; a cool, bemused appraisal that made me feel like some material object that she was considering buying or not buying.

As steadily as possible, I looked back at a heart-shaped face dominated by a pair of wide, hazel eyes. The girl had black hair, straight, and cut short above her ear lobes. Rigid bangs barely cleared a pair of thick dark eyebrows that turned up to give Gee Gee the appearance of a Mephistopheles or a pixie, depending on your outlook. I chose Mephistopheles. The effect was emphasized by high cheekbones and dispelled by a full, softly delineated mouth. She wore no makeup, although I had to look closely to determine that the round, heavy-lidded eyes, with their peculiar amber glint, were not framed by thick mascara. If Gee Gee had nothing else going for her (and certainly she had not inherited her mother's delicate beauty) she had the longest, thickest, darkest eyelashes on record. If it hadn't been for that subtly contemptuous expression, I might even have conceded that she was rather attractive.

After she had surveyed me carefully, her wide mouth curling up at one corner to indicate that I was an object of mild amusement, Gee Gee flipped over again to lie on her back. Wriggling her bare toes, addressing the ceiling in a throaty voice reminiscent of a bootleg era night club hostess, she said, 'Welcome to the cell, Warden. I just learned that I'm going to have a watchdog. Did you bring your horsewhip? Ankle chains?'

I could have been listening to a cynical forty-year-old. Still, I tried to peer beneath that hard, pseudo-sophisticated veneer. This was a child, I reminded myself. An intelligent, probably sensitive youngster who had been shunted from one boarding school to another. She had just been required to accept her fifth 'daddy.' The caustic words were just a cover-up for a little girl who was afraid of getting hurt again. I forced a friendly tone. 'I wasn't hired to play warden, Gee Gee. I'm a nurse. I'd like to be your friend.'

She released a humorless guffaw. 'Oh, wow,

is that ever a sad cliché! Who writes *your* material, Florence Nightingale?'

Psychology. I tried to recall what I had learned about reaching children who had built a wall around themselves, coming up with a blank. Inanely, I said, 'Well, if we're going to be stuck with each other, Gee Gee . . .'

'My enemies call me Genevieve,' she said curtly.

I discarded all hope of a gentle, loving approach. Perching myself on the edge of the other bed, I told Gee Gee that I had been hired to help, not to hound her. I was to see that she kept reasonable hours and followed whatever medical regimen her doctor set down for her. 'Beyond that,' I said, suddenly aware that my 'patient' was doing her best to ignore me, 'I'm about as interested in you as I am in leading a Mau Mau uprising. I'm not even obligated to try teaching you rudimentary good manners.'

'*Touchée!*' she murmured. Her tone remained one of boredom as she added, 'M.E. wouldn't like the way you talk. M.E. is exceedingly particular about my governesses. Even the amateur variety who pose as angels of mercy.'

'I'm not . . .'

'Marlaine Elizabeth has been known to crucify a headmistress for looking the other way while I went on a butterscotch sundae orgy. Firm, yes. But compassionate. For example, she nearly pulled Shadowbrook apart

33

last year because I told her my P.E. teacher had an unwholesome interest in me.' Gee Gee sprang to an upright position, staring at me with those cobra-like yellowish eyes, her voice thick with sarcasm. 'Miss Ferris, I have a devoted, conscientious mommy. It happens that I loathe her, but let's give the devil her due.'

Gee Gee not only looked reptilian; she had a forked tongue, I decided. It didn't require any additional thought to conclude that she despised her mother; she had said so, and I believed her.

Before I could offer some sort of lame excuse for Marlaine, Gee Gee snapped, 'I'm precocious. I'm the product of an emotionally unstable environment.' She threw a quick glance in my direction, probably to see if I was impressed. 'M.E. finds me enigmatic, but that's understandable. She's incredibly naive. Conversely, all of my daddies adored me.'

I began to feel sorry for the girl again. That 'all of my daddies' was a clue to the kind of instability that had produced this little weirdie. Worst of all was that sharp, defiant cynicism. As difficult as it was to generate sympathy, looking at that superior smirk on Gee Gee's face, I kept reminding myself that the kid was only sixteen. No sixteen-year-old develops a shell that impervious without having suffered deep emotional anguish. I had the impression that, in spite of her smart alec attitude, Gee

Gee Sargent had a compelling need to talk to somebody. Anybody. I folded my hands in my lap and listened patiently, swallowing my irritation.

'Stanley Sargent was absolutely mad for me. You can chalk that up to bias, if you want to. Stanley was Papa Number One. The real article, that is.' Gee Gee reached to the floor between our beds, located a cigarette pack and matches, then lighted up expertly. I had a fleeting yen to turn her over my knee as she went on, talking through a blue-gray haze of smoke. 'You've heard of Stanley Sargent?'

I hadn't, and I said as much.

'You've probably led a sheltered life. He was an actor, but he blew the Hollywood career thing, getting involved in some messy little scandal. The trial cost M. E. a fat bundle. So he's producing TV commercials and we still see each other once in a while.' Gee Gee giggled, but there was nothing girlish in that malicious sound. 'The chick he's married to currently can't tolerate my guts. Stan and I have to meet surreptitiously. Isn't that a gas?'

I was beginning to feel sick to my stomach. 'Gee Gee, it isn't necessary to . . .'

'Oh, but we ought to know each other's backgrounds if we're to have a meaningful relationship,' Gee Gee smirked. Another plume of cigarette smoke was sent ceilingward. Eyes half closed, as though she were fondly reminiscing, she said, 'After Stanley we had a whirl with Eugene Simunovich. Artist. Ascetic. Noble lineage, and all that rot. He and M.E. zapped over to Tibet to study with some creepy Lama. I was at Brandenhurst School for Young Ladies at the time.' Gee Gee raised her upswept brows to accompany the sexy innuendo in her voice. 'Learning about Life and Other Things. So I hadn't really gotten close to Gene when M.E. divorced him and we married Rex Tolhurst. Rex was unbelievably considerate.'

This was the first indication of warm human response I had heard from the girl and I encouraged it. 'You were fond of Mr. Tolhurst?'

'Oh, you're being presumptuous.' Gee Gee flicked an ash to the handwoven rug at her bedside. 'I said Rex was *considerate*. He didn't wait around to get divorced, which would have gobbled up another stack of Grandpa Kingsley's money. He very *considerately* got himself killed in a racing car. Near Rome. I was at a ranch academy in Arizona when I read about it.'

I opened my mouth to express condolences, but Gee Gee didn't pause. 'M.E. looked devastating in black. For three whole months. Then we acquired Papa Four, and was *he* a loser! Actually, I heard there was some question about Allen Montrose's gender, but don't quote me. He set up a string of spiffy hairdressing salons with the settlement money.

Isn't that handy? Whenever I'm in New York, I can get free haircuts.'

If Gee Gee expected me to echo her laughter, I disappointed her. Was she putting up a careless front by making facetious remarks about her pathetic family life, or was Gee Gee actually as calloused as she sounded? I was trying to figure her out when she puffed at the cigarette and said, 'By the way, Gestapo. Don't bother rushing over to tell M.E. I smoke. She only *pretends* not to know it, to avoid a confrontation. Where was I?' Again without waiting to be prompted, Gee Gee said, 'I was up to current *pater nútimero cinco*. Daddy Five. Not that he knew about the previous four when M.E. roped him in Las Vegas. *Am I annoying you, Miss Ferris?*'

That pointed question, expressed in a supercilious tone, must have been a reaction to the way I was looking at Gee Gee. 'I'm a nurse,' I reminded her. 'I'm not a marriage counsellor, gossip columnist, headshrinker or confessor. There's no reason for you to give me all these personal details about your mother. Frankly, I think it's in very poor taste to discuss her past.'

'Then let's talk about M.E.'s future.' Gee Gee was not in the least offended. She sounded, in fact, like a happy schoolgirl, a switch that left me completely bewildered. 'Don't you adore Noah? I absolutely flipped. He's so masculine and sexy . . .'

37

'Gee Gee, I don't think . . .'

'Baby, you'd have to be made out of concrete not to think about *him.*'

'He's a married man,' I said angrily. Gee Gee smiled knowingly at my outburst. I had sounded too defensive, and she was drawing her own, not wholly inaccurate, conclusion; I *did* think about Noah Hayden. I had found myself wishing that he weren't married, that he didn't belong to Marlaine.

As though she had read my mind, Gee Gee said in a sultry half-whisper, 'It's not as though that's a permanent condition, Nursie. I always look ahead.' The dark-lashed hazel eyes closed slowly and opened again in a parody of seductiveness. 'Noah will wise up to dear Momsy. Or some money-hungry dude will cozy up and tell her she's misunderstood.' Gee Gee turned over, dropping the cigarette into a vase full of azaleas that sat on a bedside table. I heard an exaggerated yawning sound, and then she said, 'I'm bored. Anything in your rule book that says I can't take a nap, Warden?'

I was too disgusted to reply. Although I had planned to stay, intending to address a few picture postcards of this tropical paradise to friends back home, the room suddenly became too small to hold the daughter of Marlaine Elizabeth Kingsley Sargent Simunovich Tolhurst Montrose Hayden and me.

FOUR

That was my introduction to only one of the Gee Gee Sargents. For I discovered soon afterward that there were many Gee Gees; a different personality, in fact, to suit every person and every situation.

To most of Marlaine's party, the girl was a delightfully witty, irrepressible child, sometimes given, understandably, to somber moods, which might be dispelled by appropriate gifts. Charmed by the youngster, Ernesto, our Colombian coffee millionaire, pampered Gee Gee with expensive presents, much to Noah Hayden's annoyance.

Irena, shamelessly flattered by Gee Gee, worked doggedly at casting the girl's horoscope, coming up with the startling announcement that Gee Gee was born under rare, auspicious signs usually reserved for genius, royalty, and revolutionizing religious leaders. 'The world shall hear much from our dear little Genevieve,' the bejeweled seeress told anyone willing to listen.

To Noah Hayden, who was trying valiantly to take over the paternal reins, hoping to create a family unit with himself as the sensible head of the household, Gee Gee was, alternately, a sweetly obedient little girl, and a tempting *femme fatale*. Noah was embarrassed by Gee Gee's far from little-girlish overtures; more than once I saw him firmly disengage himself from an embrace that would have been more appropriate if Gee Gee had been enacting a torrid movie love scene. He was appalled by the girl's often skimpy attire and a seductive manner that Gee Gee reserved exclusively for him, but I was sure Noah attributed these actions to an adolescent crush. Gee Gee would eventually accept him as her stepfather and friend, he must have reasoned. Meanwhile, he forced himself to be patient, to prevent an emotional explosion that would alienate the girl or cause a rift with her mother.

And Gee Gee's mother? I was sure that Gee Gee was a complete enigma to her. 'She's simply too, too much,' Marlaine would confide to me in an exasperated whisper. But the complaint, more often than not, was accompanied by an indulgent little laugh. It became obvious to me that Marlaine had been separated from her daughter too long to be able to assert any maternal authority now.

Unfortunately, Gee Gee was aware of every weakness; Marlaine's guilt complex, her consuming need to be loved by everyone, her worry about making too many wrong moves and losing her inheritance, her dread of being alone for even one minute lest she have to think or face herself, and her desire to please Noah, without giving up her friends, her way of life or her liquor. In Gee Gee's own words to me, she 'had M.E. wired,' which presumably meant that she saw through her mother and knew how to manipulate her.

Marlaine must have known who had the upper hand. No fighter, she maintained peace at any price; in her daughter's case, closing her eyes to all but the most flagrant misbehavior, busying herself with others, and probably hoping for the best. Yet, I sensed that in her confused way Marlaine loved her daughter and was saddened by the knowledge that her love would never be returned. Fortunately, she was spared a truth to which Gee Gee exposed me whenever we were alone together: Gee Gee detested her mother and actually found joy in watching her emotional turmoil.

That business of Gee Gee leveling with me was strange. She seemed unperturbed by the fact that I could only see her as a hypocrite when other people were present. She fawned over her Uncle Durwood, had him convinced that she was an adorably naive teen-ager. Yet in our room, when no one else was around and Gee Gee had finished her endless scribbling into that endless journal she kept, she would refer to her uncle with the same type of derogatory slang names she attached to everyone except Noah Hayden; 'Wall Street Willie,' 'The Adding Machine,' 'The Cube.' I wondered why she trusted me in revealing her true character. What made her so certain that

I wouldn't reveal the truth? Sometimes, trying to see into the twisted mind that lay hidden beneath her dark bangs, I wondered if this was another of the weird games Gee Gee played with people. Did she actually *hope* for a confrontation, in which the word of an adored youngster would be pitted against that of a jealous employee?

No, the more I saw of Gee Gee, the more I realized that she would not have stooped to anything that obvious. Intellectually superior, she had been left with too much time to exercise her imagination; whatever game she was playing with me, I was certain that it was as complex as her personality.

I came to another conclusion, listening to those perverse confidences. Gee Gee Sargent was completely amoral. There was no point in discussing with her the differences between good and evil; her moral code seemed to be that anything was good if it benefited Miss Genevieve Sargent. If there was one genuine emotion inside her, if she was capable of pity, affection, kindness, or remorse, it was never revealed to me. I began to find her more frightening than irritating. Yet who, except perhaps Marlaine, would have believed me if I had made such an accusation? 'Precocious, but precious' was the consensus among Marlaine's friends. Ironically, Gee Gee knew this, too, and found it amusing.

There were times when Gee Gee would

look up from her thick diary, to which she devoted at least an hour each evening, her cobra eyes fixing me with a malevolent stare, her lips subtly curved in a self-satisfied smile. I couldn't escape the thought that she was constantly planning, planning. But what? And why should it concern *me?*

Marlaine's friends had returned from the 'divorce party' that had so irritated Noah, and there had been a hectic but relatively pleasant week during which Marlaine had made a heroic effort to control her drinking and Noah had met her halfway by tagging along cheerfully on a series of impulsive jaunts to St. Kitts for a carnival, to St. Providence Island for a cocktail bash and to Martinique for no reason except that Irena had pronounced that travel was indicated in her crystal ball.

I had enjoyed the fascinating sights and sounds of each distinctively different island, and Durwood had taxed his strength to see that I missed none of the unique highlights. The others? I wondered why they bothered to fly from one corner of the earth to another when, on their arrival, they did exactly what they could have done at home. Changing costumes and emptying cocktail glasses would have been as boring in New York or Miami, it seemed to me, as in the exotic places Marlaine and her retinue chose to visit without actually seeing.

Anyway, most of the party had returned to

the villa in Port of Spain, Trinidad, where I had made Gee Gee's acquaintance. I was quartered with Gee Gee once again, though neither of us spent much time in our room. On the particular evening I remember, avoiding the perpetual party inside the house and on the terrace, I had wandered out to a secluded arbor in the garden. Carrying a tourist guide book with me, I looked forward to sitting in that bougainvillaea-covered hideaway and reading about the points of interest I might have missed in Trinidad. I learned that Durwood had found seclusion in the same spot.

'I looked for you, but you'd disappeared,' Durwood greeted me. 'Is this a coincidence, or can I flatter myself that you've been on a search for me?'

I laughed, seating myself on a bamboo settee beside Durwood. 'I cannot tell a lie. I was trying to get away from dull conversations.'

'I'll try to be scintillating,' he promised. Looking toward the villa, he shook his head in wonderment. 'You'd think they'd die of boredom, covering the same gossip over and over again. At least, with me, you can enjoy a lively discussion of the stock market. Care to hear how many points Consolidated Kumquat jumped this afternoon?'

'No, thanks. If I want to speculate, I'll consult the Countess Travalgnini. Irena can tell me how many points Consolidated

Kumquat will go up *next* month.'

Durwood shook his head again. He looked relaxed and rested, appearing younger than his age. 'Well, you wanted to see new places, meet new people. This is how the idle rich live, Roxy. Any time you're ready for a change . . .'

'It wouldn't have to be . . .' I had noticed Durwood's meaningful expression and wanted to weigh my words carefully. 'I mean, you can travel and enjoy your money without going this purposeless route. One long dull cocktail party.'

'Marlaine has to be surrounded by a crowd,' Durwood reminded me. 'We wouldn't have to be.'

I looked up to see those green eyes, that were so like Marlaine's, studying my reaction. 'We?'

'The two of us. We've had some wonderful times together on this trip, I thought. Actually, the times when we've been sightseeing or having dinner without the rest of the mob, have sold me on your idea, dear. "There's more to life than the stock market." Your words. I've gone from one extreme to the other. Now, unless you're really enjoying all these other people . . .'

'I wasn't invited to enjoy Marlaine's friends,' I said. 'This was a job, remember? A private nursing job. So far, I haven't even found out the nature of my patient's illness.'

'Neglect. Nerves, I expect.' Durwood

reached for my hand, squeezing my fingers affectionately. 'I don't think my niece would suffer any ill effects if the two of us broke away. What do you think, Roxy? Or do I have to go on for a few more months, proving that I'm not a human ticker tape?'

'You don't have to prove anything to me,' I protested. 'Durwood, I think you're the kindest, most thoughtful . . .'

On other occasions when the conversation had taken a similar turn, Durwood had taken me off the hook by admitting that he was too old for me, too staid, too conservative. Now, recovered from his illness and convinced that my arguments about his inability to enjoy life had been beaten down, he pulled me close to him, closing me in a tight embrace.

It was strange. As parched as I was for love, I felt no response to that expert kiss. It was like being kissed goodbye at a railroad station by an older brother, except that it lasted longer and was not a farewell but, in Durwood's mind, a beginning.

I knew that his own ardor had blinded Durwood to my indifference. 'We've waited far too long, darling,' he murmured. His lips were pressed against my forehead as he spoke. 'I love you, Roxy. I'd like to take care of you for the rest of your life. See to it that you realize every one of those romantic daydreams of yours.'

I was searching for a way to tell him that

nothing had changed, that I still regarded him as a purely platonic friend, almost a paternal figure, when loud voices from the garden interrupted.

'. . . tired of your ugly accusations!' The angry voice belonged, unmistakably, to Marlaine. Durwood released me from his embrace, startled by the sound.

Evidently Noah and his wife had started their argument on the terrace and had decided to pursue it in a more private spot. They stopped no more than a few feet from the gazebo-like structure in which Durwood and I had found seclusion, separated from our view by a towering row of hibiscus bushes.

'. . . sick of having you follow me around like a nursemaid, telling me what to do and what not to do,' Marlaine was shrilling. 'You were abominably rude to Wesley just now. He's . . .'

'He's lucky I didn't break him in two.' Noah's anger matched Marlaine's. 'I don't want that leech hanging around you.'

'At least he treats me like a woman, not a . . . not a retarded child.'

'He treats you like a future meal ticket!' Noah raged. 'Even your daughter sees it. Everyone knows he's just waiting around for you to get drunk enough and for me to get disgusted enough . . .'

'Go ahead! Leave me! I'm used to it! I know better than to expect a man to love me for what I am.'

Durwood cringed at the sobbing note that had crept into his cousin's voice. Marlaine had been drinking, which was not unusual. But now she sounded pitifully drunk and near tears. He was as reluctant to eavesdrop as I was, yet making our presence known would have been embarrassing to all of us. We sat quietly, breathing hard, hoping the couple would pass by without seeing us.

'Don't you see, it's *because* I love you that I can't let you go on this way.' Noah had taken on a warmer, patient tone. 'You know I didn't marry you for your money. I didn't know you *had* money. I couldn't care less. Marlaine? Honey, listen to me . . .'

'You despise me,' she was crying. 'You hate my little girl . . .'

'I don't hate anyone. Marlaine, try to understand . . . if I didn't care about you, I wouldn't care what that kid does.'

'You accused her of being . . .'

'I said she's not behaving like a normal sixteen-year-old. Okay, she's had too much emotional upheaval. I want to be a father to her. Not a . . .'

'Go on! Say it!' Marlaine shrieked the challenge. She was close to hysteria.

'I'll say this. The next time she throws herself at me, the way she did just now in the sun room, I'm going to . . .'

'You're going to *what*?'

Noah sounded deflated as he said, 'I don't

know what I can do except get your cooperation, Marlaine. Talk to her. Set her an example. My God, let's get away from all these phonies and start living like a man and wife, people with a huge responsibility. The girl needs a home. Let's make one for her. Let me get back to a medical practice, settle down . . .'

'You promised.' Marlaine was weeping like an injured child now. 'You said you'd let me have this one last wonderful time. And I've tried so hard, Noah. I skipped Lucy's party, just to please you. But you won't even try to be civil to my friends. You can't stand to see me happy. You're like my damned puritanical father . . .'

Marlaine and Noah had evidently resumed their walk, for their voices receded with their footsteps until Marlaine's tearful complaints were inaudible.

Durwood, who loathed emotional displays, was too shaken by the incident to continue his own pursuit. His face flushed, barely able to look at me, he muttered, 'Nothing more uncomfortable than having to overhear something that personal.'

I nodded, sympathetic with Durwood's embarrassment. Marlaine was, after all, a member of his family. 'It's a . . . rather sad situation.' We started out of the blossom-covered bower, headed back toward the house, peering ahead cautiously to make sure we would avoid the quarreling couple. 'They're

49

both people I like. I wish.'

'Wish you could mediate, but you feel it's not your business?' Durwood asked.

'I guess that's it. They're neither of them happy, of course. It seems to me they could be, if . . .'

'I don't like getting involved,' Durwood said unnecessarily. (As though a financially independent bachelor had to tell me that he had always lived for himself, skirting emotional entanglements, and, except for his quasi-proposal just a few minutes ago, avoiding even the responsibilities that go with loving someone else!) 'But . . . perhaps I should do the cousinly thing. At least express my opinion, short of offering advice.'

Knowing Durwood's sensible attitudes, I would have sworn that he meant having a heart-to-heart chat with Marlaine, backing up Noah's demands, advising her to stop running, stop drinking, begin being a wife and mother. It was inconsistent with Durwood's philosophy for him to think otherwise. But evidently I had placed more value on Durwood's conservatism than on his family loyalty. In a controversy between a Kingsley and an outsider, his sympathy was with the Kingsley. At least it seemed that way to me when he said, astoundingly, 'Noah's being entirely too dictatorial. He knew he wasn't marrying a prim hausfrau. It's unjust to expect Marlaine to make a drastic change in her way of living.'

I was too shocked to make any comment. But not nearly as stunned as I was, seconds later, as we neared the terrace to see Gee Gee, scantily clad in the barest excuse for a dress, stretched out on one of the lounge chairs, watching our approach with that pleased expression I had learned to dread. I had no doubt that she had watched her mother and Noah going out to the garden, knowing the two of them were racked by conflicting emotions, with even greater satisfaction.

'I may have to talk to Noah about his hostile attitude toward that child,' I heard Durwood say. 'Gee Gee's so responsive to kindness that he hasn't anyone to blame except himself if they don't get along.'

'But she resents . . .' I had started to blurt out the truth; that Gee Gee was jealous of her mother, that her interest in Noah was rejected because it was far from being wholesome.

'Gee Gee doesn't resent Noah at all,' Durwood said, completely misinterpreting what I was going to say. 'She's heartbroken about the way he's rejected her.' Durwood sighed, lowering his voice as we drew closer to the subject of our conversation. 'Such a sweet, bright youngster. I hate to see her being hurt because an adult is so insensitive. Seeing Marlaine all torn up, too.' He stopped talking, leaving the impression that he would have to become involved, distasteful as it might be.

It wasn't until later that evening that the

unsavory afterthought sprang into my mind: could Durwood have a selfish motive in encouraging Marlaine's dissolute life, or her permissiveness with Gee Gee? Everything I knew about Durwood pointed to his agreeing with Noah's stand; he was another man who I thought would have sympathized with Noah's attitude. If Marlaine was encouraged, would she alienate her father completely, along with the Kingsley millions? Durwood had said that the old man respected him. If Marlaine were cut out of old Mr. Kingsley's will, would Durwood be a possible heir?

It was an ugly thought, and probably grossly unfair to the man I, too, had learned to respect. Yet what other explanation could there be for Durwood's topsy-turvy viewpoint?

I didn't dwell on the question long. Partly because I was ashamed of myself for mistrusting someone who had been uniformly kind to me and only a short time ago had declared his love for me. Partly because of that. But mostly because I had a conversation several hours later that made me wonder if my own thoughts and desires were above reproach. Close to midnight, I had my first long dialogue with Noah Hayden.

FIVE

Thinking about the Haydens' problems, and Durwood's unexpected reaction to them, I had half forgotten my own dilemma. Sooner or later, Durwood would resume the dialogue that had been cut short, and I would have to tell him that his efforts to 'prove himself' hadn't changed my mind. He would be hurt, of course, and the situation would become unbearably sticky.

Going to the room I shared with Gee Gee served as a reminder that I couldn't stay on my present 'job' in any event; Gee Gee looked the picture of physical health as she sprawled on her bed feigning sleep. (Pretending that she was asleep whenever she chose not to talk to me was another game that Gee Gee played.) But I couldn't vouch for her mental health; I knew that I was neither qualified nor inclined to serve as a private psychiatric nurse. No, there was no question about it; I would have to drop out of Marlaine's entourage and return to New York.

Uncomfortable in the room, with Gee Gee's eyelids fluttering occasionally as she stole a glance to see what I was doing, I was equally reluctant to go downstairs, where the nightly party was just getting into full swing. Durwood had retired to his room, following his doctor's orders to get plenty of rest, so there was no chance of running into him if I left the room. I decided to walk down to the beach, where I could think out my next move without being distracted.

Ironically, as I crossed the wide expanse of lawn that would take me to the beachfront cabanas and hammocks, I was thinking about Noah, and my reluctance to leave and never see him again, when I heard him call my name.

I spun around to see Noah hurrying to catch up with me. A full moon filtered through the tropical garden, blanketing the scene with a pale, silvery light; Noah was clearly visible as he closed the distance between us. 'Mind having company?' he asked. 'I was thinking about a walk along the beach myself.'

More thrilled than I had any right to be, I welcomed him to come along. We walked quietly for a few yards, followed by a hubbub of voices from the terrace. As we reached the sand, taking time to slip out of our shoes and leave them on the porch rail of a bamboo dressing room, Marlaine's unmistakable laughter, high pitched and, somehow, unmerry, cut through the balmy night air. After that, strolling along sand that was still warm from the afternoon sun, I was aware of no sounds except those of the gentle surf and the padding of our footsteps.

For a long time, skirting the water's edge and heading, as if by agreement, for a palm-studded cove about a half mile from the villa, Noah and I discussed trivialities; the high humidity, the lovely flowering trees and shrubs banking an estate next to the one we were occupying, the phosphorescent glow of the whitecaps reflecting the moonlight.

I don't know exactly how we started talking about ourselves. I think Noah said something about the southern part of his home state, California, boasting a great number of the exotic plants that were so impressive to me. Yes, that was how it began. I had spent most of my life in a climate where tropical plants couldn't survive, and, somehow, we got to talking about New York, the hospitals he knew about there, and . . .

And, perhaps inescapably, because the wound had not yet healed, but also because I was feeling particularly isolated from my own kind of people that night, weary of conversations and problems that had nothing to do with me, and desperately in need of a sympathetic ear, I found myself perched on a driftwood log, telling Noah all about myself. About myself and Bill Hardin and the bitter blow that had been dealt to my ego.

'It's just my ego, though,' I admitted finally. 'I mean, I can't say my heart is broken, or anything as traumatic as that. I don't even dislike Bill for what he did, anymore. He just realized he didn't want to be married, to me or anyone else.'

Noah was pensive for a long while before he said, 'People have a way of making those decisions too soon or . . . too late.'

'I'm not sure I follow you,' I told him. 'I guess you mean I was lucky that Bill changed his mind before we were married. It would have been worse after we'd started a family.'

'That's true,' Noah agreed. 'A guy who can go through a couple of years of the medical school grind and then drop it is liable to have a change of heart about anything. But I wasn't referring to your case.' His mouth twisted in a melancholy grin. 'Self-centered. I was talking about myself.'

I didn't want to encourage personal revelations that he might later regret having made. After the unhappy scene with Marlaine, I had probably caught him in a regretful mood; tomorrow Noah would resent my knowing too much about his marriage. So I didn't ask him to go on. I didn't have to.

'About making the wrong decisions too soon,' he went on as though I had invited the confession. 'I was engaged to marry a girl . . . up until just a few months ago.'

I frowned. 'I thought you met Marlaine just before . . .'

'Not Marlaine,' he said solemnly. 'Her name doesn't matter. I was insanely in love, we had set a date, both sets of parents were delighted. Her father and my dad shared a practice in Pasadena. Still do. I had just joined the medical complex, after six years of clinical service, so it was all very cozy. One big happy family.'

Noah picked up a broken shell, toyed with it for a moment and then hurled it back to the sand. 'You'd have to know how perfect everything was—what an ideal, beautiful future I had laid out for myself, to understand why I went berserk when it all exploded.'

'Something happened?' I asked tenuously.

'An accident,' Noah said. 'Plane crash.' Before I could offer condolences, assuming that the girl he loved had been killed, Noah added, 'No one was seriously hurt, except me. And I wasn't even in the plane.'

I frowned. 'You aren't getting through to me, I'm afraid.'

'The private plane belonged to a man Peggy had dated before she met me. The two of them were taking off on their way back from a rendezvous up at Lake Tahoe when it happened. Freak accident; smashed into a jeep on the runway. It was unusual enough to hit the papers. So I woke up one morning to see my future wife's picture on the third page, along with her lover boy's.' Noah sighed. 'Peg was supposed to have been visiting her aunt in San Francisco. Shopping for her trousseau. She didn't even bother to deny that she'd been "making sure she wasn't making a mistake" in marrying me.'

'I can almost appreciate what Bill did, now,'

I said. 'At least he was honest with me.'

'Right. Maybe we were both fortunate.' Noah made a shrugging gesture. 'The difference is that you went right on working, keeping yourself busy. I went flying off to Las Vegas, about as close to being insane as it's possible to get without flipping out permanently. I drank myself into what I hoped would be an anaesthetic stupor. A good idea, except for the fact that sooner or later you've got to sober up.'

'Which you did,' I said, guessing the rest.

'And when I saw daylight again, I was a married man.' Hastily, Noah added, 'This isn't a complaint, understand. Marlaine's a wonderful person. Once she realizes that someone actually loves her . . .'

Noah left the sentence hanging. He had said nothing about the shock he must have experienced in learning that he was Marlaine's fifth husband, that she was the mother of an extremely precocious child, that she was the shaky heiress to a vast fortune. If he had heard these facts from Marlaine during their whirlwind romance in Nevada's plush gambling resort, their full significance hadn't hit until later. And now he seemed desperately anxious to convince me, and perhaps himself, that he had not made a tragic mistake.

'I must belong to another century,' he said after a long pause. 'My attitudes toward marriage and divorce aren't fashionable anymore. Besides, I . . . I'm convinced that all Marlaine and I have to do is change the atmosphere around us. This . . .' He waved, vaguely, indicating the villa and the people crowded into it. 'This isn't conducive to the kind of home life I want for my wife or for myself. It's going to have to change—and soon.'

We talked, then, about the kind of existence we considered ideal. It wasn't much of a coincidence to discover that we shared the same general goals; most people in the world would have agreed with us. But, somehow, with our shared interest in medical matters added to the more average daydreams, we both sensed a rapport that had no right to exist. Noah seemed actually embarrassed when he said, 'We have an amazing lot in common.'

I nodded slowly. 'Yes.' Was he thinking, as I was, that we were almost ideally suited to each other? Or that he and Marlaine had not one shred of mutual interest, that nothing in their backgrounds should have drawn them together, nothing about their life styles promised to hold their marriage intact? Even without the added harassment of Gee Gee, once their brief physical attraction for each other wore off, what could they look forward to?

A soft breeze rustled through the palm fronds, echoing the rhythmic hush of the surf. I could have attributed Noah's attraction for me to any of a variety of influences. We were alone together in a romantic cove of a romantic island; the moon was full and breathtakingly close; the warm air was scented with the perfume of exotic tropical blossoms. There were all these made-to-order factors, plus my sympathy for Noah's situation, my respect for the way he refused to admit that he was ensnared in a trap, blaming no one but himself when he hinted it was a terrible mistake, letting me know in no uncertain terms that he was determined to make a go of his marriage and asking for no sympathy.

I wasn't a woman Noah had turned to for the cocktail lounge brand of 'understanding'; he had done that once and he was prepared to pay the price for it. Yet I sensed—no, I *knew*—that the powerful force that drew me to Noah was not something that I felt alone. It was a mutual magnetism; he was aware of it, too.

So aware, that he became suddenly nervous and irritable. 'I don't know what we're doing here,' he said, getting to his feet abruptly. 'I ought to be keeping an eye on my wife.'

Politely, I refrained from mentioning Wesley Reed. After her spat with Noah, Marlaine would be easy prey for Wesley's 'consolation.' I made some inane remark about too much liquor being bad for people, especially someone as high-strung as Noah's wife.

The walk back toward the villa was tense

and near silent, each of us locked in our private thoughts, neither of us giving voice to a rapport that was painfully obvious. If Noah had accidentally touched my hand, if we had exchanged only a few words that expressed the way we felt, I would have been in Noah's arms.

Stopping to get our shoes, we were almost curt with each other, as though we couldn't wait to break away from this impossible situation and run. If the mixture of emotions that churned my insides could have been defined, I would have said that I was angry, bitterly angry, with a fate that had led me to fall in love with a man far beyond my reach. For I realized, during that nerve-racking return to the house, that my ill-fated romance with Bill Hardin was no more than an adolescent crush. It had been no more than a dress rehearsal for the real thing. This was love, and the pain of it was more than I could endure.

We parted on the terrace with deceptively casual goodnights, and Noah went inside the house in search of his wife. Because I was hopeful that Gee Gee would be genuinely asleep by then, and because I wanted nothing more than to pull a cover over my head and blot out my awareness of Noah, I returned to my room.

I showered and changed into pajamas, moving quietly so as not to disturb Gee Gee, who *was*, it seemed, fast asleep. As I crept to my bed, a strong intuition that I was being watched came over me. I looked up, instinct warning me that I would meet the reptilian stare that had chilled me so many times before.

I was not wrong. There was no light in the room except a wide patch of moonlight, cut into wavy-bordered squares by the latticework grille covering the seaward windows. The square of eerie light fell over Gee Gee's bed, illuminating her face and throwing strange shadows over the mound of pillows on which her head was propped. She was smiling, always a frightening sign, because Gee Gee only smiled when she was trying to charm someone or when one of the pawns in whatever game she was playing had made a wrong move.

I had seen the latter smile before; when Marlaine drank too much and Noah annoyed her with a lecture, when I made a *faux pas* that raised the eyebrows of Marlaine's super-sophisticated friends, or when Gee Gee glanced up from recording the day's events in her voluminous record book. I shouldn't have reacted as I did, but I had never seen a more ominous expression in those strangely yellow eyes.

My startled gasp was exactly what Gee Gee had hoped for. The smug grin widened and she purred, 'Something bothering your conscience, Warden? I didn't think you'd jump like a scared rabbit if I simply looked at you.'

'My *conscience?*'

My defensive tone was also pleasing to Gee Gee. 'Heavens to Betsy, but we *are* edgy tonight, aren't we? I didn't accuse you of anything, Nursie.' She waited until I had gotten into bed, pulling a woven cover over my shoulders, not only to ward off the chill of an overactive air conditioner, but because, for some unaccountable and infuriating reason, I had started to shiver. I was trying to ignore Gee Gee, annoyed with myself for not being as cool and self-controlled as this incredible monster of a kid, when she said, 'Fabulous night for a walk down the beach, isn't it, Roxy?'

She sounded so friendly, so *sincere!* It was the first time she had ever addressed me by my first name, and for a moment I thought *maybe the strong facade is breaking down; she's just a mixed-up child who's been putting up a nasty front because she's afraid of getting hurt again. If she gets a warm response, if I treat her like the love-starved youngster she is, maybe . . .*

I was wrong again. I had forgotten that I was in the presence of an adolescent genius, and probably the world's most gifted actress. 'M.E. wouldn't appreciate your going for long moonlit walks with her latest.'

I started a bristling reply, but when Gee Gee had something to say, she didn't allow an interruption. 'For that matter,' she continued, '*I* don't like it, Gestapo . . . and that should be

63

considerably more impressive. Genevieve didn't like it one *bit.* Dig?'

I had just made up my mind that I wasn't going to tolerate this humiliating situation one more day, so it didn't matter what I said to Gee Gee. If I recall correctly, I turned my back on her and said, 'You disgust me.'

She giggled; a menacing, vindictive giggle that showed she was pleased with my reaction. Then, in the sweet, little-girl tone that she reserved for her mother's friends, she said, ' 'Cause I love my nice daddy. I wouldn't want anyone to take him away.' The facetious tone gave way to a husky murmur that might have been meant for me, but sounded more like Gee Gee communicating with herself: 'I love my daddy so much, I'm not going to divvy him up with *anybody.*'

SIX

I gave Marlaine my notice the next afternoon. She got up shortly after noon to discover that Noah had gone for a solitary walk early in the morning and hadn't returned. I had to wait until she consulted with her 'psychic adviser,' Irena, and breakfasted, with Wesley Reed, on oatmeal (because Irena had advised 'attention to diet and matters of health') and cuba libres (because Marlaine had 'got up with an insatiable thirst for rum and Coke'.)

When Marlaine's dapper Lothario had reluctantly gone off to play tennis with the French actress, Bunny Stafford, and Tish Vandercourt, Marlaine sent one of the servants to summon me to the rooms she shared with Noah.

Marlaine rested on a leopardskin-covered chaise longue, and was in the process of lighting one cigarette from another as I came into the jungle-style living room of the Haydens' second-floor suite.

Wearing an emerald-green toreador suit with a frilly white blouse and flaming red cummerbund, she looked dazzling, if one ignored the lines of dissipation under her eyes and the shakiness of her slender fingers. As I seated myself on the sumptuous couch Marlaine had indicated with a wave of her hand, she asked, 'Gee Gee still asleep?'

I nodded. 'I think so. She was when I left the room.'

Marlaine groped blindly for a cocktail glass on the table at her side, found it, and then said, 'I don't suppose I can offer you a drink?' She shrugged off my polite refusal. 'Okay, darling. I had an idea this was going to be a business consultation instead of a social call. What is it, Roxy? My little girl giving you a hard time?'

The words were pronounced in a careless manner, but the pained expression in

Marlaine's eyes kept me from telling her that, yes, her daughter was not only giving me 'a hard time', she was totally intolerable. I decided to place the blame for my decision elsewhere. 'It's just that I feel superfluous, Marlaine. No one's told me what Gee Gee's problem is. Assuming she *has* a problem that calls for full-time nursing care, and I doubt that, I haven't been told what I'm supposed to be doing for her. Frankly, I'm beginning to feel guilty, too.'

'*Guilty?*' Marlaine nearly spilled her drink as she whooped out the word.

'You'd have to understand how desperately nurses are needed,' I explained. Looking at Marlaine's uncomprehending expression, I knew she was incapable of understanding labor shortages or guilt over neglecting the serious purpose of my profession, let alone the fulfillment that comes with doing an important job and doing it well. She had never worked a day in her life, and once I had heard her wondering aloud why the servants 'would want to work so hard at such utterly dreary jobs.'

There was no point in giving her a short course in economics or dedication. I settled for saying, 'I don't think Gee Gee really needs a nurse.'

'Well, I'm glad to hear that, of course,' Marlaine said airily. 'I tried to tell that to the headmistresses of her last two schools, but you know how stubborn old maids can be. You'd think they'd take the word of a competent doctor. I'd had Gee Gee checked over, a complete physical, just before I enrolled her at Shadowbrook. And then the silly dean has the audacity to refuse Gee Gee's application for next term because she's ill. *"Very sick."* ' Marlaine imitated a mincing tone. 'She wanted to have one of her boring consultations with me.'

I was beginning to suspect that Gee Gee's teachers and I, having spent more time with the girl than Marlaine did, and making our observations while sober, had reached similar conclusions. Hesitantly, I asked if Marlaine had had the requested meeting with the dean.

'I couldn't have made it, with all the commitments I had at the time,' Marlaine told me. She sounded a bit incredulous; wasn't it unthinkable that she should be expected to miss out on a series of 'madly divine' parties, just because some 'dreary female' wanted to tell her some unpleasant facts about her daughter? Marlaine didn't want to be inconvenienced with the truth. It wouldn't have helped one iota if I had told her what I thought about Gee Gee.

'She can be a trial,' Marlaine admitted. 'But I suppose you have to expect that with exceptionally brilliant kids. She has a fantastic I.Q., you know. Somewhere in the genius vicinity; isn't that *mad?* But then, Stanley Sargent is a brain. Impossible to live with, but

67

I'd never deny that Gee Gee's father is one of the most intelligent . . .'

Marlaine dropped the sentence in mid-air, emptying her glass and losing interest in the subject. I hadn't come to discuss the sterling qualities of her past husbands. I had come to give my notice, and I took advantage of the pause to tell Marlaine. 'So . . . since we're agreed that Gee Gee doesn't need an R.N., I'd like to make arrangements to get back to New York as soon as possible.'

It apparently hadn't dawned on Marlaine, until that moment, that I actually wanted to quit my job.

'But, darling, that's absurd!' she protested. 'New York's absolutely grisly at this time of the year. A slush heap. And all the fun things are just coming up. The most fabulous cruise . . .'

'I'm sorry,' I said. 'I've had a vacation. Now I've got to get back to work.'

'Durwood's going to be crushed,' Marlaine went on. 'He adores you. And here I thought you were having a lovely time. Dear, would it help if I had a chat with Gee Gee? If she's been consuming too much of your time . . . you know I can always send her to Grandpa's place for a while. My father thinks the sun rises and sets with Gee Gee, which is unfathomable, considering how straight-laced he is, but she seems to have a way with him. She adjusts beautifully while she's with him.' Marlaine giggled, totally oblivious to the ridiculousness of her proposition. She was telling a nurse that the 'patient' could be sent elsewhere if that would make the job more appealing! She was equally unconcerned about Gee Gee's ability to 'adjust' to a puritanical old man. Evidently it didn't occur to her that Gee Gee was a born liar and a gifted hypocrite, faking a deceitful personality with anyone from whom there was something to be gained.

'I think Gee Gee's place is with you,' I said. It was the most tactful way that I could remind Marlaine that her daughter's problems stemmed from being shuttled from one place to another. 'She'll enjoy this vacation with you, and then you and Noah will be establishing a permanent home for . . .'

'Don't let's talk about that permanent home nonsense,' Marlaine cut in. 'I get too depressed. Can't you just see me having the PTA ladies in for tea and worrying about the Girl Scout car pool?' She lifted her eyes ceilingward and released an exasperated sigh. 'I might have to go through the motions, to humor my father and Noah, but the thought of living in some suburban mausoleum . . . I'd perish. I would absolutely perish from boredom.'

Confused by Marlaine's grasshopper mind, finding it almost impossible to stick to my original reason for requesting this meeting, I made another attempt to convince Marlaine that I wanted to leave, and soon.

She looked at me mournfully, her lovely green eyes misting over. 'I'm so disappointed, darling. I feel that I've failed you.'

'But you didn't . .'

'You wouldn't dream of leaving us if you were enjoying yourself,' Marlaine insisted. 'Why don't you just forget about Gee Gee for a week or so and let Durwood zip you to St. Kitts? There's the most marvelous little inn there where . . .'

'Marlaine . . . I didn't come here to . . .'

'Oh, if you're concerned about your reputation, I can loan you a chaperone.' Marlaine laughed, reaching for a fresh cigarette. 'Irena's been dying to do some shopping at St. Kitts. I'll rent her out to you, how's that? Mother Marlaine's Handy-Dandy Rent-a-Chaperone-Service. Because, darling, we both know Durwood arranged this little hiatus because he's simply mad for you, and you could do a lot worse, believe me, child. Take the advice of a five-time loser, Durwood's perfect husband material. He was getting a trifle stuffy there for a while, but this trip's done wonders for him. I mean, he's really tried to be a fun person, and, as he told me when we decided to invite you along, you're mad about traveling and meeting new people. It's all in the palm of your little hand, darling, and you can't be serious about leaving Dur and going back to some dismal hospital to carry bed pans.'

70

I sat listening, stunned, while Marlaine made it crystal clear that my 'nursing job' had been a flimsy pretense. Either Marlaine had had too much to drink, or she felt safe in telling me that Gee Gee's 'nervous condition' had been a hype. (Though, ironically, I agreed with the dean from that fashionable school who had called Gee Gee 'very sick.') I felt that I had been lied to and used, and suddenly my disgust with rich people who thought they could buy whatever they wanted, flared up in resentment. 'Marlaine, I have no intention of marrying your cousin. I told him that before we left New York and I'm going to tell him again, as gently and as firmly as possible.' Getting to my feet, I softened my tone, aware of Marlaine's incipient tears. I had to keep remembering that Marlaine's whole existence centered around everyone's adoring her, and wanting to be with her. From her distorted viewpoint, I wasn't merely quitting a job that had never existed, I was rejecting Marlaine herself! 'I've had a . . . wonderful time,' I assured her. 'You couldn't have been nicer to me, but . . . it's not fair to encourage Durwood when I . . .'

'You are truly the sweetest, most selfless creature on this planet,' Marlaine announced. Her eyes looked glassy now, but she leaped up from the longue, suddenly animated. 'I loathe seeing you go, dear, but I'm so impressed. Anyone as considerate as you deserves a

71

glorious, glorious send-off. Roxy, we are going to stage a farewell party to end all farewell parties!'

I was too bewildered by the sudden shift in moods to notice that the door had opened behind me until Marlaine looked over my shoulder to greet her husband. 'Noah—darling, Roxy's decided to fly off to grubby old New York to do her nurse thing and I can't talk her out of it. So what we've decided to do is . . . that is, if your persuasive powers fail . . . we've decided to have a gigantic, grand, *memorable* bash, to see her off properly. Trul' mem'rble.' Marlaine had started slurring her words, and the last phrase was barely understandable.

'I see.' I turned to see the grim expression on Noah's face, a look that matched his terse voice. He barely noticed me, looking instead at Marlaine's tottering effort to cross the room as she carried her glass toward a bar in the corner.

Marlaine must have sensed Noah's mood. She appeared to be having trouble in maintaining her carefree, madcap attitude; she was making a concentrated effort to walk in a straight line. 'Sweetie, aren't you going t' . . . c'vince Roxy that she shoul'n leave us? Talk to her in that in'mitable bedside manner o' yours.' Marlaine nearly lost her footing as she looked back to wink at me. 'Noah's doctor, y'know. All doctors have besside manner.'

Noah's face had gone white. Without a word, he crossed the room, intercepting Marlaine before she reached the bar and yanking the glass out of her hand. 'I'd advise anybody I know to get as far away from this stinking atmosphere as possible.' Noah's growling words were accompanied by the smashing of crystal on tile as he hurled Marlaine's glass to the floor.

I edged toward the door, wanting no part of another embarrassing domestic spat. But instead of an angry outburst, Marlaine reacted by throwing her arms around Noah, clinging to him like someone drowning. 'I'm sorry,' she said. 'Promised you I wouldn' drink all day. Honey, please don't be angry. *I need you so much.*'

No one who cared about Marlaine could have resisted that soul-racked plea. For an instant, Noah stood rigid, still shaken by anger. Then, as the plaintive appeal was repeated, I saw his muscles relaxing, his eyes taking on a compassionate softness, his arms enveloping Marlaine as though he were protecting a sobbing child. 'Try not to drink, honey,' I heard him murmur. 'You don't *have* to drink anymore. Look, *I love* you. You don't need any of those creeps downstairs . . . you don't have to keep running. *I love* you.'

It was what I wanted to hear, for Marlaine's sake, but the words were too painful for me to listen to. I had no right to wish that Noah were saying them to me. I wanted only to race from the room.

Marlaine was crying in her husband's arms, and I would be crying in another minute, too, if I didn't escape. I was going out the door when I realized that my own tears, as well as my love for Noah, came from a deeper wellspring than Marlaine's. As I left the room, I heard her whimpering, 'I'll try to be good, Noah. I really will. If you'll just let me give this one li'l party for Durwood's li'l friend . . . 'cause she's *so* sweet. I could abs'lutely *kill* Gee Gee for making Roxy want to leave . . .'

SEVEN

Marlaine, as usual, prevailed. The Haydens' farewell party for me was held in a Port of Spain night club that Marlaine had taken over—restaurant, dance floor, stage, and bar —for the night. Where the party-goers who crowded the club had come from eluded me; I didn't know that many people, and certainly there weren't that many who wanted to wish one Roxy Ferris, R.N., bon voyage. My departure was just one more excuse for the jet set to gather, and the party was just one more feather in Marlaine's social cap.

A carnival atmosphere prevailed, confetti

74

and smoke filled the air, and apparently there were uncounted broken hearts because I was leaving; certainly the bar was dispensing enough booze to console the relatives of an overseas-bound battalion. Somehow, the Bunnies and Tishes and Ernestos were cheered by the libations. The only miserable expressions around were those of Noah Hayden, Durwood Kingsley, and myself.

Since I had told him of my decision, Durwood had virtually stopped talking to me, behaving as though I had gone back on a solemn promise. I had given up trying to convince him that it was quite possible to like and respect a man without wanting to spend the rest of your life with him, that my refusal to marry him was not a personal affront. It was hopeless. Durwood Kingsley, who had probably never brooded before, chose to feel hurt and rejected and there was no dissuading him. He sat in a dim corner of the main room, half hidden by a table piled high with gifts for me, gloomily listening to the Countess Travalgnini, who was undoubtedly explaining his bad fortune in terms of planetary positions. Irena, so bejeweled for the occasion that she probably couldn't stand up because of the weight, had developed a consuming interest in Durwood. Unfortunately, he had not gazed into the same crystal ball that had told the seeress her destiny would be intertwined with that of a bachelor broker nearly twenty years

75

her junior; Durwood looked as though he wished Irena would disappear in a puff of smoke.

Noah's misery was less obvious. He was keeping his end of the bargain with Marlaine, going through the motions of a party-giving host. You had to look into those deep blue eyes of his to see the mingled sorrow and concern.

For Marlaine was hardly fulfilling *her* part of their agreement. Dazzling in a brightly printed sarong-like costume that left her white shoulders bare, her red hair worn loose, she was not only the most attractive and animated woman at the party; she was easily the most giddy from champagne. I had seen Noah whispering to her several times, smiling and trying not to appear like a stern parent spoiling a child's fun. His patient efforts at slowing her down were not succeeding. The inevitable next step would be an angry rebuke, and I knew that Noah was anxious to avoid the public scene that would result.

With his wife the scintillating center around which had gathered a sycophantic crew Noah detested, he was as lost in that crowd as I was.

And I was lost. Guest of honor I might have been, but I felt too melancholy to enjoy the few people who remembered that this was a gala send-off for 'dear Gee Gee's darling little nurse.' A few, like the coffee baron from Colombia, had added to my depression by being patronizing. How wonderful democracy was, Ernesto reminded me. In his country it would have been unheard of for a servant to be honored with an expensive party. Gee Gee, who had been included among the adult guests, was present to overhear the remark. Knowing exactly how I felt, she agreed with Ernesto that democracy was certainly wonderful. 'But, then, my mother is *exceptionally* democratic,' she pointed out sweetly. 'She's generous with *everybody*.'

It was a double-edged insult, aimed as much at Marlaine as at me. (Marlaine was being 'generous,' at the moment, with Wesley Reed, as everyone could see.)

I could almost hear Gee Gee's inward simpering as my face colored. I was too disgusted to reply. After all, what did it matter? In a few days I would be gone. Hopefully, I would never see any of these people again. I would forget . . .

It struck me, then, that there was someone else I would never see again. And I wasn't likely to forget Noah. I was convinced of that when the two of us found ourselves alone together shortly after the incident with Ernesto. Feeling sorry for myself, I told Noah what had been said.

'Damned wealthy parasites,' he muttered. 'They look down their noses at anyone who works for a living.' We were standing near the periphery of a circular glass dance floor,

77

lighted from underneath with a kaleidoscope of changing colors. A popular combo that Marlaine had had flown over from New Orleans ('because the locals play everything as though it were calypso') finished a raucous jazz number and slid into a sentimental standard from the thirties. Noah gestured toward the dance floor. 'Shall we? This is about my speed.'

I was in his arms, then, following Noah's easy steps, hoping that he wouldn't feel the accelerated pounding of my heart as he held me close to him. Just before he had asked me to dance, we had opened up a subject of conversation in which we had mutual interests. We could have gone on discussing the jet set, their purposeless lives, the restless dissatisfaction that kept them racing around the world looking for an elusive happiness that they might have found in productive work. We could have talked about Noah's consuming need to resume his medical practice, about his plans to go back to California for just that purpose. He might have touched upon the fact that we had interests, goals, and standards in common. One of us might even have suggested that it was a pity we had met too late.

Was Noah thinking of this, too? And was that the reason for his silence as we danced? The magnetism that I had sensed on the beach was present again, as palpable as the hard lump in my throat. It seemed that everything we had to say to each other could not be said, yet was understood by both of us.

Noah was solemn and I was near tears as our dance ended. Walking from the dance floor, which now glowed an appropriate shade of blue, I caught Gee Gee's meaningful stare. She was seated at a stageside table with a callow youth of about her own age, but the escort that had been chosen for her (one of Tish Vandercourt's nephews, I think) held little interest for Marlaine's daughter. She smiled seductively at Noah, the smile becoming baleful as she returned her attention to me, and then we had passed her and it was over. Still, I felt Gee Gee's eyes on my back as Noah guided me to a secluded table.

We sat down and a waiter appeared instantly, like a conjured genie, with two champagne-filled glasses. Noah lifted his in a toast. 'To happy times, wherever you're going, Roxy.'

I clinked my glass against his, cursing myself inwardly for rising tears that threatened to make a public spectacle of me. I forced a devil-may-care tone. 'Cheers. And happy times to you, wherever *you're* going.'

Noah sipped from his glass, scowled at it, and set it down. 'You know, when you see the way booze has messed up the lives of people you know, you begin to wonder if Carry Nation didn't have a point.'

I was afraid of saying the wrong thing, so I

just sat there with what I'm sure was an insipid half-smile on my face.

'This crowd couldn't function without it,' Noah went on, 'so don't worry. I address my temperance speeches only to members of my immediate family. Marlaine and myself.'

'Yourself?' I had rarely seen Noah drink anything stronger than dinner wine.

'Yes. We amateurs have to be especially careful. Especially around the old pro boozehounds.'

Noah was trying to sound light-hearted, but I could have bet that he was remembering a night in Las Vegas when he drank with an 'old pro boozehound,' waking up to find the entire course of his life altered. If he was looking back with regret, he changed the subject quickly. 'So you're going back to the city. Got something lined up? A job . . . future husband?'

'I told you about my luck with future husbands. Nothing like that.'

'You'll be going back to work, then. Where?'

'Oh . . . wherever the registry sends me.' I pondered the possibilities for a moment. Oddly, I hadn't given any thought to exactly what I would do. 'I think I'll go to work in a hospital. General duty. Private cases are . . .' I shrugged. 'I don't know. You get too involved.'

Unconsciously, Noah glanced toward the table where Durwood was still puffing on his pipe, a new habit he had acquired to keep from smoking cigarettes, and listening to Irena rattle. 'You've managed to get uninvolved.' The somber blue eyes met mine, leaving me breathless for a moment. 'You're very fortunate,' Noah said quietly. 'It should be that easy for everyone.' He was skating on thin ice again, and Noah made another abrupt shift. 'Have you heard the latest? We're going on a cruise. Four weeks on the Caribbean, with absolutely no liquor and no leeches aboard. At the end of four weeks, we head for New Orleans and from there Marlaine and Gee Gee and I are flying to L.A. A month from now I'll be caring for patients again. Funny, it sounds like paradise to me. And I'm supposedly in a vacation paradise now.'

'I don't think people can be happy unless they feel productive,' I said. 'I miss working. That does sound crazy, doesn't it? I remember telling Durwood that if I could afford it, I'd do nothing but travel and have fun. And now I . . .'

'Noah, you promised you'd dance with me.'

Gee Gee's plaintive little-girl voice stabbed into our conversation. She had apparently ditched her young escort and had appeared next to our table. In the dim light, she may have gone unnoticed for several minutes, and I had a startled moment in which to wonder what Noah and I had been saying to each other and how much of it Gee Gee

81

had overheard.

'I don't want to interrupt you,' Gee Gee went on, sounding like a model of schoolgirl deportment. 'But Mums says I have to go back to the villa pretty soon and that awful Roger has two left feet. I wanted to have *one* other person dance with me before I leave.'

Gee Gee's adolescent plea, coupled with the demur blue cotton frock she had chosen to wear (an incredible contrast with the slinky, abbreviated dresses that made up most of her wardrobe) left Noah no choice but to treat her like a child who has come to her first grown-up party only to find it disappointing. He was gracious, if not paternal. 'I'm afraid you'll find that Roger and I took dancing lessons from the same teacher,' Noah said. 'But I *did* promise, didn't I?'

'Gosh, I don't like to be a pest,' Gee Gee apologized. Under the black fringe of bangs, her eyes were wide with innocence. 'If you'd rather stay here with Miss Ferris, I . . . I won't really mind.'

Fantastic! She could have won an Oscar for that blend of courtesy and shattered hope. Noah gave me a wan smile. 'Miss Ferris understands,' he said gently. He got to his feet, trying not to appear reluctant. 'Will you excuse me, Roxy? You won't be bored. The band's due for one of those stomping numbers and you can sit here and watch me make an idiot of myself.'

Gee Gee emitted a schoolgirl giggle and linked her arm through Noah's possessively. 'You're both awfully sweet to me,' she said. Noah couldn't possibly have seen the look of triumph she threw back at me as he guided her to the dance floor.

I would have preferred to sit out the dance alone. But as the band fulfilled Noah's prediction, breaking into a jumping rock number, and as Gee Gee swung into a rhythmic gyration that belied her pose of prim childhood, Wesley Reed found his way to my table.

I don't usually have strong reactions to people I don't care for; I avoid them, if possible, and tolerate them when they can't be avoided. However, Wesley Reed, like Gee Gee, was an exception. His mere presence gave me a skin-crawling sensation, and I was sure that this feeling was mutual. Yet as he took over the chair that Noah had been occupying, that dapper creature was unusually affable. 'Inexcusable to leave the guest of honor sitting here alone,' he said. I was sure that he practiced that oily tone and the pseudo-sexy stare while alone, in front of his bathroom mirror. 'Especially such a pretty guest of honor.'

I made some sort of polite remark while Wesley made a production number of taking a cigarette from a gold case engraved with his initials and inserting it into a ridiculously long and ornate gold holder. The maneuver was as pretentious as the mod dinner jacket and the yellow paisley ascot tie he affected. I caught a whiff of an expensive spicy cologne, advertised to make the male irresistible to women. What did he want? I wondered. It wasn't like Wesley to tear himself away from Marlaine to keep me company.

I got a hint of what he wanted quickly enough, for although Wesley made a fetish of appearing 'cool' at all times, he was eager for information and he wanted to waste as little time with me as possible. 'The monster drag your boy away?' he asked. Before I could object, he said, 'Roxy, dear girl, let's not pretend that you don't see through that intolerable offspring of Marlaine's. You and I, being outsiders wanting in, have to be particularly astute. Little Genevieve may have everyone else fooled, but the two of us *do* know she's a monster. As for your boy . . .'

'I don't know who you're talking about, but if you're referring to . . .'

My irate protest was brushed aside with a languid wave of Wesley's cigarette holder. 'Look, love, we can be honest with each other. We may dislike each other . . . a form of professional jealousy, perhaps . . . but we do share the same aspirations.'

'I didn't know that I shared any aspirations with you,' I told him icily.

'Oh, come off it, Roxy. You didn't come

along on this safari to be a ministering angel to that insufferable brat. Though I will say that I lost a little respect for your judgment when you changed your mind about bagging Dur Kingsley.'

'I never intended to . . .'

'I can only attribute your change of heart to a condition which I deplore in others and consider too luxurious for myself.' Wesley's pencil-thin moustache wriggled in amusement and he feigned a deep sigh. 'True love. I can't begin to afford it. But, then, you haven't had time to acquire my taste for the costlier things in life.'

I started to get up. 'I don't know what you're talking about, but if you're implying . . .'

Wesley waved me down. 'Dear girl, don't let a bit of blunt honesty upset you. Surely we can level with each other?'

I sat, open-mouthed, as Wesley made it clear that he considered me a sister member in his fortune-hunters' society. There was nothing I could say to convince him that I hadn't maneuvered to 'land' Durwood Kingsley for purely financial reasons. There was even less chance of convincing him that I wasn't madly in love with Noah Hayden. Maybe my arguments about Noah were less convincing because, in this case, Wesley was absolutely right.

'I won't say you've been obvious,' he told me in a reassuring tone. 'Remember that I've had years of practice observing who's out to get whom. A matter of self-preservation, really. Knowing other people's plans is often advantageous in promoting my own.'

I glared at him, but Wesley was undisturbed. Although I was too irritated to give him my full attention, I gathered from his sly hints that he not only suspected, but actually *hoped*, that Noah and I were caught up in a raging love affair and that Noah would be leaving for New York when I did! My furious denial must have been persuasive. 'All right, he isn't going to go dashing off with you this week, but anyone can see he doesn't fit in with Marlaine's friends. Or with Marlaine, for that matter. It's inevitable that they're going to split up sooner or later. And, of course, it would help me to know.' Wesley smiled at me as though I were a fellow-conspirator. 'We impoverished peasants can only invest so much time and money in a project, as you know.'

It would have been a waste of effort to tell Wesley what I thought of him or of his shoddy values. Instead, I had the satisfaction of reminding him that Marlaine's father wouldn't take kindly to another divorce and another marriage, if that was what Wesley was waiting for.

He was not that easily dissuaded. Furthermore, Wesley had given that aspect of his pursuit considerable thought. 'These things take time,' he said through a slowly puffed billow of aromatic tobacco smoke. He turned his sleepy-eyed gaze to the dance floor, where Noah was evidently having trouble disengaging himself from a hold that Gee Gee hadn't learned in dancing classes at one of those elegant schools for young ladies. 'Ah, well, if I can't count on your cooperation, dear girl, I can certainly count on *hers.* If Genevieve doesn't send Dr. Hayden running for freedom, nothing will.'

'She's Marlaine's daughter,' I reminded him. 'Assuming that you succeed in breaking up the marriage, what do you propose to do about Gee Gee?'

Wesley went through the motions of a bored yawn before he murmured, 'A cage would be eminently suitable.' He must have noticed Marlaine's approach before I did, because the cynical mask on his face changed instantly to a suave, adoring half-smile and I heard him purr, 'Sweetness, where've you been *hiding?* I was about to send out a Saint Bernard with a cask of rum.'

Her walk shaky, in spite of flat sandals, Marlaine held out both her arms in greeting, crying, 'The prodigal daughter hath returned from the little girls' room. Hullo, Roxy. Darling, you look absolutely ravishing tonight. Wes, I *told* you my phony eyelashes were ready to fall into my drink.'

'Poor child,' Wesley cooed.

Marlaine had leaned down to throw her

arms around him from behind his chair. 'I waited and waited for you to send the rescue team. I haven't had a drink in . . .'

'You've had far too many.'

The three of us snapped to attention at the rough sound of Noah's voice.

Marlaine straightened up, taking her arms from around Wesley's neck. 'Never mind the Saint Bernard,' she groaned. 'My watchdog's on the scene.' She had tried to make a joke of the interruption, but seeing Noah's livid face had frightened her. 'I saw you dancing with Gee Gee, dear. You can't know how happy I am to see the two of you so close.'

'Too close for comfort,' Noah snapped. I had never before seen him more furious. 'Damn it, I can't blame her for acting like a cheap floozy. You're her mother. If you were setting her a decent example . . . if you'd taken the trouble to notice that she's been swilling champagne all evening, trying to keep up with you . . .'

Noah's voice had risen to a loud pitch and several people had stopped their conversations to stare at him.

'Baby, you don't want to make a scene,' Marlaine whispered.

'I can't top you when it comes to public spectacles,' Noah roared. 'Or that kid. I can't even repeat what she just said to me. It's the first time I've been propositioned by a sixteen-year-old kid.'

88

'Honey, you know Gee Gee's terribly mature for her age,' Marlaine said. She was making a valiant attempt to sound calm. 'So maybe she has a crush on you . . . it's perfectly understandable.'

Wesley had got up out of his chair. 'You've gotten yourself terribly upset, Noah, old boy. What say we all meander over to the bar and cool ourselves off?'

Noah, who had lost control of himself completely, was raging his opinion of that idea when Durwood came hurrying over to our table. Scowling, he addressed Noah in an angry, but still dignified, monotone. 'Noah, this is intolerable. I just ran into Gee Gee and the poor child's hysterical. She said you'd humiliated her. What in the name of heaven's gotten into you?'

Marlaine was suddenly filled with maternal concern. 'Where did she go? Poor thing, I'll have to talk to her.'

'She was going to get a cab,' Durwood said. 'I couldn't stop her.' He placed a consoling arm around his cousin. 'I think I'll get back to the house. Marlaine, Gee Gee shouldn't be left alone in that condition.' He looked daggers at Noah. 'I can't imagine anyone hurting a child the way she was hurt. I'll go see what I can do for her.'

Noah started to reply, but Durwood was on his way out of the club, and Marlaine was calling out after him, *Would* you do that,

89

Durwood? I can't possibly leave my guests and I hate to think . . . if she's despondent . . .'

'She isn't despondent!' Noah yelled. 'She's a neurotic brat, and she needs attention, Mother. So let's get back to the house and . . .'

'You're spoiling everything,' Marlaine wailed. 'Oh, Noah, how can you be so cruel? *Roxy's party!* This is Roxy's farewell party and you want me to . . .'

'I want you to start acting like . . .'

'People, *please!*' Wesley made an exasperated gesture. 'The press is here, you know. Let's go have that drink and let everyone cool down. Unless you want a juicy scandal reported on the society pages . . .'

'I couldn't care less.' Noah reached out to take Marlaine's arm. 'Let's go, Marlaine. Roxy won't object.' He looked toward me for corroboration, and I nodded. 'I'm sure she agrees that your daughter needs your attention more than this mob.'

Marlaine pulled away from his touch, turning to Wesley. 'Wes, you understand, don't you? Tell him to stop bullying me.'

Wesley looked as though he were torn between avoiding a confrontation with Noah and taking advantage of an opportunity that would make him a hero in Marlaine's eyes. As Noah and Marlaine shouted at each other, Wesley apparently decided to place his bet on the latter course. Putting an arm around Marlaine's bare shoulders in a protective pose,

90

he said, 'Don't worry about this brute, darling. He and your little nurse are in such *perfect* agreement that he shouldn't be around to torture you much longer.'

I don't know how Noah could have heard that statement, above his own demands that his wife accompany him, and Marlaine's pleas that she simply couldn't leave her own party. For that matter, maybe Noah didn't hear the actual words. Wesley's insinuating tone, and the intimate manner in which his fingers pressed into Marlaine's upper arm, were all that Noah needed to trigger an explosion that had been long suppressed.

It happened before anyone could move to stop Noah or to shout a warning. His right arm swung out in a wide arc, his fist crashing into Wesley's jaw. Marlaine screamed as Wesley's arm left her shoulder. He toppled backward, the fall of his body broken by a table, then a chair, before it thudded to the floor. The blow and the fall were accompanied by the blinding light of a photographer's flashbulb.

After that, there was bedlam; guests screaming, Marlaine astounding everyone by ignoring the fallen hero and sobbing that Noah had spoiled the party, waiters and the club manager converging on the scene, and more flashbulbs popping.

Noah just stood there for a moment, breathing hard and looking at the small trickle of blood oozing from Wesley's open mouth.

The latter had been knocked unconscious, and it was strange that no one except Noah and me showed any concern for Wesley's condition.

Muttering 'I shouldn't have done that,' Noah reverted from outraged husband to attending physician, kneeling down beside his victim to assess the damage.

I found a pitcher of water on one of the tables, soaked a napkin, and offered Noah a cold compress. Apparently this was enough to revive Wesley. He shuddered, half opened his eyes, groaned and spat out a mouthful of blood. While Noah checked for broken bones, Wesley shoved him away and started dragging himself to his feet, making a blubbering, incoherent noise.

Another brouhaha erupted in the circle surrounding us. I caught a glimpse of Irena, her jeweled fists pounding on the back of a press photographer as she shrilled, 'Get out of here! Give me that film, you . . . vulture . . . stop taking pictures!'

Several other guests, conscious of bad publicity for reasons of their own, joined the melee. I saw the photographer racing for the door, his precious camera clutched against his body as though it were a football, while another young man, probably a reporter from the same paper, ran interference for him like a blocking back at a football game.

In the midst of all this chaos, the excitable British manager of the club leaped to a table and shouted a nervous plea for calmness. Under other circumstances, I would have found his attempt hilariously funny. He was trembling like a malaria patient, so unnerved that he stuttered his words. 'It's all qu-quite all right, l-ladies and g-gentlemen. Please r-resume enj-joying yourselves. N-no harm d-done. N-n-nothing serious, you know . . .'

His services as a doctor rejected, Noah turned to me and said quietly, 'I'm afraid I managed to loosen a couple of teeth, Roxy. I don't know if you want to clean him up. Might be better to call a doctor.'

Wesley, using a silk handkerchief to blot his mouth, was making his way to the men's room, trying to muster up as much dignity as possible. Although he was not especially popular with Marlaine's other friends, most of whom regarded him as a socially inferior opportunist, I would have expected someone to show concern for him. The guests seemed more interested in gossiping about the incident than in comforting Wesley. I offered first aid, but was rewarded with a poisonous glare as Wesley brushed past me.

Marlaine was the one who amazed me. A moment ago she had been asking Wesley to rescue her from a brutish husband. Now, either because she was impressed with Noah's manly approach, or because she feared a scandal that would reach her father's attention, she was suddenly the obliging wife and distraught mother, a heavy combination to juggle considering that she was barely able to stand on her feet. 'Should pro'ly see 'bout Gee Gee,' she slurred. Noah helped her to the door and I followed, suspecting that he would need help.

Maybe it was discretion, maybe it was indifference, but no one paid any attention to our exit. We filed past the table on which my unopened bon voyage gifts were heaped, and minutes later, with Noah on one side and me on the other, Marlaine slumped down in the taxi seat and passed out.

'I think the party's over,' Noah said to no one in particular. From his resigned tone, I guessed that he was referring to more than the 'fantastic farewell party to end all farewell parties' his wife had planned for me.

EIGHT

Marlaine, blissfully out of the picture, was carried to her bed by Noah and one of the servants. I preceded them up the stairs of the villa, meeting Durwood in the hallway.

Normally self-possessed, he was now extremely agitated. 'Thank goodness you're here,' he greeted me. 'I can't do a thing with Gee Gee. I think she's seriously ill.' I noticed that Durwood's shirt had been ripped. His hair looked mussed as though he had just been through a physical struggle. He took time to shake his head as Noah and Marlaine's personal maid carried their unconscious burden past him. Then, addressing Noah, Durwood said, 'Can you come into the room—and see what you can do? It's terrible . . . the poor child's having convulsions! I couldn't restrain her!'

As Noah promised to look in as soon as Marlaine had been tucked into bed, I opened the door to the room I shared with Gee Gee.

It was an indescribable sight. Nothing that wasn't nailed down had remained in place. It was as though a maniac had torn through the room in a wild orgy of destruction. Glass from a set of framed Chinese prints littered the floor. The prints themselves were in shreds, the bamboo frames splintered. One ceramic lamp had been smashed, and the shades of two others had been reduced to confetti.

My wardrobe trunk stood open, its contents ripped and strewn around the room. Both beds appeared as though they had been attacked with a sharp instrument. Both of the lovely handloomed covers were heaped in a mound on my bed, and it looked as if a fire had been started in one of the depressions, for a large black hole had been burned through several layers of fabric. Sheets had been slashed to ribbons, clear through to the mattress covers. Gee Gee was lying in the center of her bed, her eyes pressed shut, writhing like someone in the midst of an epileptic seizure.

Durwood had followed me into the room, his voice trembling with awe. 'She had done most of this before I even got here. What is it? It was like trying to control a . . .'

Durwood stopped, reluctant to pin the label of insanity on his niece. He was close to tears, unnerved by the ordeal, yet relieved by the arrival of professional help.

I crossed the room to Gee Gee's bedside, checking for symptoms of a convulsive seizure. There were no indications of body rigidity, no signs of eye rolling, tongue biting, or frothing at the mouth. Besides, if Gee Gee were an epileptic, I certainly would have been advised of the fact. She did not feel or appear feverish, though she was breathing heavily and her heartbeat was abnormally fast. Still, her manic activity during the last twenty minutes or so would have accounted for this.

Noah came into the room while I was checking Gee Gee's pulse. With Durwood hovering over him anxiously, Noah made a quick examination. Once, after lifting his eyes to survey the debris around him, Noah looked at me as if he was sharing my conclusion: we were dealing with an emotionally unstable girl who had been called down for her behavior. Frustrated because she hadn't been able to have her way, Gee Gee had found release in a violent temper tantrum.

Durwood caught the exchange of glances. 'What is it?' he asked. 'Is there something you can do for her?'

'I doubt it,' Noah said gravely. 'I'm afraid Gee Gee will have to be hospitalized.'

Durwood's eyes bulged. 'It's that bad?'

'Usually, in extreme cases of this type,' Noah went on, his eyes fixed on Gee Gee's fluttering eyelids, 'the patient requires institutional care. Occasionally, for the patient's own protection, surgical correction is indicated.'

Durwood swallowed the bait intended for Gee Gee. 'You aren't talking about a . . . *lobotomy?*'

'I certainly hope that won't be necessary . . .' Noah left the impression that he had serious doubts. 'Of course, unless we see a marked improvement . . .'

There was an agonized sound from Gee Gee and she opened her eyes. 'Uncle Dur, don't let them send me away,' she cried. She sat up, fully conscious, reaching out for Durwood's hand. 'They hate me. They all hate me. Did you hear what he just said? He wants to lock me up in some horrible asylum . . . cut out a part of my *brain!*'

Durwood dropped to the edge of the bed, putting his arms around his niece, stiffly uncomfortable. 'Nothing's going to happen to you, dear. It's all going to be all right.'

Gee Gee buried her head in his shoulder,

sobbing piteously. 'I'm so unhappy . . . I wish
. . . I wish I was dead!'

Durwood glared at Noah. 'Did you have to
frighten the child?' He patted Gee Gee's
shoulder awkwardly. 'I'll see that nothing bad
happens to you, honey. Come on, now. Don't
cry.'

Gee Gee only increased her choking cries.
'W-why did Mumsy marry him? I thought . . . I
thought . . . she'd . . start to like me . . . but . . .
all he does is . . . he turns her ag-against me.'

Durwood made a half-hearted attempt to
assure Gee Gee that she was loved, but he was
obviously finding the emotional display
upsetting. Accustomed to his orderly bachelor
existence, Marlaine's cousin was probably
wishing he had never got involved with her
domestic complications. He was torn between
envy and resentment when Noah excused
himself from the room for a moment, and as
Gee Gee worked herself up to shrill hysteria.

While I waited for Noah to come back, my
mind whirled with confusion. Gee Gee's
feeling of rejection was valid; her need to
strike out was understandable. She might have
been faking the 'convulsions' and the coma,
but no child could have emerged from her
background unscarred, so an outburst of some
kind, at some time, was inevitable.

At the same time, I had an intuitive feeling
that I was not in the presence of an emotion-
racked, love-starved adolescent. *I was watching*

and listening to a diabolically clever performer giving her impression of the way a love-starved adolescent would behave. It was an eerie sensation, like watching a human being's caricature of a human being. I could have been observing an android or an alien from another planet who has studied humanoid emotions and learned to imitate them, using the talent to manipulate these same emotion-bound creatures.

Yet how unjust, how heartless it would be, I thought, to cling to this bizarre theory and show indifference to a child's suffering! A mentally disturbed patient might be crafty, might even feign tears for a purpose, but this didn't make the patient well. Only a thoroughly miserable youngster would seek attention with destruction and hysteria.

Gee Gee added terror to her gamut of emotions when Noah came back to the room with a sedative. She refused to take the two tablets, clinging to Durwood and begging him to save her from being 'doped or poisoned.'

When her uncle was reaching the point of exasperation in trying to overcome this paranoic reaction, Gee Gee shifted to mewling little-girl tears and apologies. And her attention was focused on Noah.

'I'm . . . sorry,' she wept. (Who could have doubted her sincerity?) 'I didn't mean . . . all those terrible things I said. I just . . . want you to . . . *like* me, Noah. I never had a daddy who liked me.'

I saw Noah's eyes mist over, and I knew he was castigating himself for not understanding the girl's inner confusion, for handling a touchy situation badly. In a hoarse voice, he assured Gee Gee that he liked her . . . that he wanted to love her as though he were her own father.

Gee Gee threw her arms around *him*, then, leaving Durwood free to escape with a mumbled excuse about needing to lie down and rest. Actually, I hadn't thought about the strain that had been placed on his heart while he had tried to stop Gee Gee's fit of destruction.

'I . . . shouldn't have . . . wrecked everything,' she wept now. 'I know you don't . . . hate me, Noah. You've even . . . tried to get Mumsy to . . . to . . .'

'She loves you very much,' Noah said. 'Look, we'll talk about it in the morning, Gee Gee. The three of us. Like a family, okay? Right now you're exhausted, so you take these pills and get a good night's sleep, all right? Will you do that for me?'

She nodded like an obedient five-year-old and gulped the pills and the water Noah provided for her. 'I made so much . . . trouble for you,' Gee Gee said to me as I made an attempt to straighten her bed.

I followed Noah's lead, speaking with all the affection I could muster. 'It's all right, Gee

Gee. I don't know where the linens are kept and we don't want to wake any of the help. Tomorrow we'll straighten out the room and . . .'

'I'll pay for everything I wrecked,' Gee Gee promised in a touchingly remorseful tone. 'Out of my allowance. Only my . . . mother's going to hate me. This isn't even our house.' She nestled her head back on the pillow I had plumped for her. 'I've never . . . had my own room. Just . . . dorms and . . .'

'We won't tell your mother, and you'll have a room of your own,' Noah said.

'You're so nice to me, and I was so awful . . .'

'Get to sleep now.' Noah's face creased in a kindly smile. 'We'll get everything all squared away tomorrow.'

'My Mom won't . . . come in here now . . . and see this mess?'

'No, she's asleep,' Noah said.

'Did she . . . pass out?'

Noah colored at the poignant, embarrassing question. 'No, no . . . she was just very tired, Gee Gee.' There was an awkward pause and Noah started to walk away from the bed.

'Would you . . . do me a . . . big favor?' Gee Gee half whispered.

Noah turned back. 'If I can. What is it?'

'I know I don't deserve it, but . . .' Gee Gee swallowed hard, as if to muster up courage. 'Would you . . . kiss me goodnight?'

Noah's color deepened, but he smiled gently

101

and said, 'Sure.' He leaned down to plant an equally gentle kiss on Gee Gee's forehead, patted her upper arm and told her goodnight. Gee Gee rewarded him with an adoring look, and then closed her eyes. She looked blissful, almost angelic, in spite of her tear-splotched face.

I walked out of the room with Noah, telling Gee Gee I would be back in a minute. In the hallway, with the door closed, I asked, 'Any instructions, Doctor?'

He pursed his lips, releasing a soft, sighing whistle. 'Just try to keep your cool, Nurse. She should be asleep soon. Try to get some rest yourself.'

'I thought you handled that rather well,' I told him.

'You mean, calling her bluff?' Noah moved away from the door, lowering his voice. 'I had a hunch she was faking that . . . catatonic state. But that explosion that preceded it must have been for real. Poor Durwood.' Noah sighed again. 'Now I'm beginning to feel guilty about being as rough with the kid as I was. She can't help being mixed-up. Over and above the usual adolescent turbulence.'

'No, I . . . felt very sorry for her tonight,' I admitted. 'Though, frankly, I . . .'

Noah's eyes met mine as I cut my sentence short. 'Yes?'

'She bewilders me, Noah. If she weren't so all-fired clever . . .'

'That brassy front she puts up?' Noah made a disparaging grimace. 'That's a thin shell, Roxy. She ran some of her frustrations out tonight. Scared herself, probably. Now she's sorry, and that pseudo-sophisticated wall's been cracked. Inside, she's just a lonely little kid. Did you hear that remark about never having a room of her own? A home. That's what she was talking about. A home, with parents who love her enough to make her tow the line. Can you even begin to visualize the kid's insecurity?'

'I hope you'll be able to change that, Noah.' Unconsciously, my glance drifted to the door behind which Marlaine slept her drunken sleep. 'For everyone's sake.'

'We're going to make some drastic changes in the morning,' Noah said fervently. 'Maybe we made the breakthrough tonight.'

'Could very well be.'

'Will you be able to manage? The kid made quite a mess of the place.'

'Oh, I'll get by, thanks.' There was a momentary silence during which the powerful rapport that existed between us was so overwhelming that I felt faint. Noah started to say something, then evidently changed his mind. I ended the impasse by saying goodnight.

'Goodnight, Roxy,' he said. 'Thanks for the help.' Another pause, and this time Noah's gaze drifted from one closed door to another,

103

his eyes reflecting the sorrow he refused to express. Then his mouth twisted in that now familiar wry grin of his and he said, 'I'm sorry about your farewell party.' He was halfway down the hall when I heard him add, 'I'm sorry about the farewell, too.'

I stood motionless for a few seconds. Then, before melancholy could fasten its grip on me, I hurried back to the disordered bedroom.

Gee Gee appeared to be asleep. Because I was too unnerved for sleep myself, I busied myself for a while picking up the larger pieces of glass and removing the fine splinters from the area near our beds with a damp towel. I spent another few minutes trying to make my bed with what was left of the linens.

By the time I had washed and found a nightgown in the piles of clothing that had been dumped out of my suitcases and drawers, I was tired enough, I thought, to sleep. But I lay awake, reviewing fragments of the disastrous evening, fighting off thoughts of Noah by reminding myself that I had once been obsessed with thoughts of Bill Hardin, too, and now he was only a vague memory, someone whose face I could barely recall. If I had loved Bill, then I had recovered; in time, I would forget Noah Hayden, too.

I had left the bathroom light on, with the door slightly ajar, concerned about Gee Gee getting up at night and stumbling over some of the broken objects that I hadn't yet picked up.

It was by this dim light that I saw the quaking motion of Gee Gee's shoulders as I turned over in my bed. She was absolutely quiet, even her breathing was soundless, and I had assumed that she was sound asleep. Yet the spasmodic shaking of her upper body alarmed me. Was she sobbing quietly, too ashamed to let me hear or witness her misery?

I remembered what Noah had said; Gee Gee's brassiness was just the cover-up of a bewildered, lonely kid. Guilty because I had failed to recognize this simple truth, I swung my feet to the floor in the space between our beds. As tenderly as possible I placed a hand on the girl's shoulder and whispered, 'Gee Gee? There's nothing to cry about, honey.' The shaking continued under my touch. 'Nobody's angry with you,' I went on softly. 'Tomorrow morning you're going to start a whole new way of living.'

I kept talking, telling Gee Gee that she was fortunate in having a kind, understanding stepfather who loved her and wanted to make a home for her. I spun the idealistic dream of a home in California, a loving mother who would be at home each day when Gee Gee came home from school. It would be a regular day school, where Gee Gee would make permanent friends; they would go to the beach together, visit each others' homes, talk about boyfriends during pajama parties in Gee Gee's very own room. For there would be boys at the high school, too. It wouldn't be an isolated boarding school for girls. California was a teen-agers' paradise. 'Maybe you'll get one of the boys to teach you to surf . . .'

I kept talking, talking, painting the hopeful picture that might have excited me if I had been sixteen and I had been deprived of a normal childhood. The trembling was still going on under my fingers, and I wondered, dismally, if the trauma was so severe that Gee Gee no longer believed in, could not imagine or project herself into a happy family life. 'It's going to be wonderful, Gee Gee,' I said. 'You don't have any more reason to cry.'

She turned over then. And I don't think I ever experienced a more stabbing shock. Her face was contorted, not with tears, but with laughter . . . the most perverted, malevolent laughter imaginable. In the semi-darkness, her yellowish eyes glowed with that contemptuous amusement I had seen before, but this time Gee Gee could barely control herself. 'You . . .' My breath congealed in my lungs as she tried to stop her soundless laughter enough to speak. 'Ferris Wheel, you are . . . you are . . . absolutely . . . unbelievable. You are . . . you are just . . . just too, too much.'

I withdrew my hand, falling back toward my bed. She was laughing aloud, hysterically triumphant, as I pulled the tattered covers over my head. *Poor Noah*, I thought. My own humiliation, my own fright at being in the presence of something abnormal and incomprehensible, took second place. Poor Noah. Loving stepfather, devoted husband. Going by the rules in Psychology I book, planning a home, building a marriage, building a family around this core of evil!

I shuddered, listening to the now audible delight of Marlaine's precocious baby. The pills Noah had given to Gee Gee took effect perhaps ten minutes later and the subdued laughter ended. *(Poor Noah. God help you, Noah. Noah, I love you.)* The first pink glow of daylight came through the windows before sleep overcame me.

NINE

I will never know why I didn't tell Noah and Durwood about my experience with Gee Gee that night. A tragedy might have been averted; all of our lives might have been different as a result.

Maybe it was the nightmarish quality of that insane laughter that led me to keep it a secret; the whole evening had been like a bad dream, and, perhaps defensively, or because I knew that I would soon be escaping the situation, I chose to put it out of my mind.

I slept late, but I preceded everyone else to the breakfast tables that had been laid out on the terrace. Marlaine's friends had evidently kept the party going until dawn; there was no sign of the other houseguests. But the Hayden-Kingsley clan, Marlaine, Noah, Gee Gee and Durwood were awake (in fact, Gee Gee was missing from her bed when I got up), for the maid who served my papaya juice, scrambled eggs, and coffee informed me that they were all sequestered in the Haydens' suite upstairs, with orders that they were not to be disturbed. I gathered that a serious family meeting was in progress.

They emerged shortly before noon, the four of them seeking me out in the library, where I was using the phone to make plane reservations. They were all smiling, rested, eager to convey the results of the pow-wow that had been going on for several hours.

'We want to talk to you, darling,' Marlaine began. Her arm was linked through Noah's, her slender fingers intertwined with his.

Durwood smiled at me for the first time since his proposal had been rejected. Gee Gee plucked at the cap sleeves of my denim sports dress (an outfit I had never worn before, and the only thing Gee Gee had missed in ripping through my closet), pursed her lips and said admiringly, 'Mm . . . that's sharp! How come you don't wear blue more often, Roxy . . . it's so neato on a blonde.'

Yes, and I remember Noah looking like a shy bridegroom with a message to convey. All of them together forming the friendly, handsome, ideal All-American family that you see in those impossible magazine ads, admiring their new carpeting or beaming at the new air conditioner.

For once, Marlaine let her husband take the lead. Dutifully quiet, casting adoring glances at Noah and sometimes nodding her agreement, she sat next to him on one of the library's settees, with Gee Gee curled at their feet, while Noah detailed for me the results of their family conference.

'We're anxious to get back to the States and settle down,' he told me, 'but after all the . . hectic goings-on, we've decided that we could all use a little quiet relaxation. Give us a chance to get better acquainted as a family, for one thing.'

'And we think of you as family, darling,' Marlaine interjected.

Durwood held a match to his pipe, nodding. He blew out the flame and said, 'It would be a shame for you to come all the way out here and not see all the islands, Roxy. This cruise Marlaine had lined up will take us to Haiti and then Caracas . . .'

'Oh, it sounds *dreamy*,' Gee Gee said. I think I could have talked to her about surfing high school boys in California at that moment and seen her go into adolescent ecstasies.

'Then, there's the practical consideration,' Marlaine added. The Kingsley heiress, who had never had a practical thought in her life, pointed out that the thousands of dollars she had paid out to charter the luxury yacht were not refundable. 'I'd hate to think of all that hard-earned money going down the drain,' she said.

Noah winced at the 'hard-earned' phrase, before going on to tell me that everyone had agreed it wouldn't be a fun cruise if I weren't along. I listened to a barrage of persuasive arguments from all three of the adults, collectively, and later, individually. Noah, Marlaine, and Durwood, when they spoke to me privately, each placed emphasis upon my 'stabilizing influence.'

Gee Gee needed a young woman she could emulate, Durwood said. If he still had a more personal motive in talking me into taking the cruise, it was not mentioned. 'You must have done wonders, talking to Gee Gee last night,' he complimented. 'I was ready to leave for home myself, after that incredible scene with the kid. She's a changed person today. Told her mother that you had a long heart-to-heart chat with her before she went to sleep. They're so grateful to you, Roxy. I think they'd be crushed if you left them now.'

I had reservations about the results of that 'heart-to-heart chat,' but then my ego pushed common sense out of the way. Maybe I *had* managed to reach Gee Gee, after all. She had been too proud to admit it to me, hence the ridiculing laughter, but suppose Durwood was right? It was a formidable challenge; I would perform an invaluable service for the Haydens if, during a peaceful cruise, with Marlaine separated from liquor and her dissolute friends, with all of us devoting time to Gee Gee, I could effect a dramatic change in the girl's outlook.

By the time Noah and Marlaine had talked to me, I was beginning to think of myself as a combined psychiatrist and good Samaritan. And then Gee Gee added her personal plea: 'I know I've been awful, Roxy, but I'll just die if you don't come along. I resented you, at first. You know . . . I thought you were going to be like all the jail keepers I had over me at the boarding schools. Last night . . . well, you were so cool, I guess I realized you're just about the best friend I've ever had.'

That did it. I saw myself as a heroine, a psychological genius, a miracle worker. While the cruise itself was extremely appealing, it was conceit that dictated my decision. The Haydens were delighted. Durwood gave me a paternal squeeze and said he knew I wouldn't let him down. And Gee Gee? If she wasn't sincere, she certainly gave a good imitation of being overjoyed.

To celebrate, Durwood took us out to dinner that evening. It was like the new beginning Noah had promised Gee Gee. There were no jet set characters to compete with for her mother's attention. Marlaine confined herself to one daiquiri before our sumptuous lobster dinner, and while we listened to calypso singers, enjoying the view of tropical gardens and the sea from the restaurant's terrace, strangers might have taken us for an ordinary family group of tourists.

Gee Gee glowed with girlish enthusiasm, and after our waiter had carried a tray of exotic flaming desserts to our table, a flamboyant surprise arranged by Durwood, Gee Gee said, 'Everything's been so *perfect* tonight, hasn't it? I don't mean just the fabulous dinner and everything.' She looked starry-eyed, and even her manner of speaking was less brittle, more naive. 'I mean . . . being with my four very favorite people.'

Marlaine reached across the table to give her daughter's hand an affectionate squeeze. 'You'll have favorite people aboard the yacht for a whole month, darling.'

'Nobody else?' Gee Gee questioned.

'Well, a crew would be nice,' Noah said. I had never seen him in better spirits. 'Unless you want me to take charge. I once rented a rowboat, if you want my qualifications.'

Gee Gee laughed. 'No, silly. I mean . . . no other guests?'

'Just family,' Marlaine assured her.

'Not even . . . you know who?'

Gee Gee had not been told that Wesley

112

Reed had been flattened by her new stepfather the night before. If she had overheard gossip from the other houseguests during the afternoon, or if she had seen the servants removing Wesley's luggage and sending it to the airport, it seemed to me that she would have assumed that Wesley was now *persona non grata.*

'*Especially* not you-know-who,' Noah said firmly. 'Your mother and I told you that earlier, Gee Gee. We aren't taking any guests.'

Marlaine's face clouded for a moment as she toyed with her dessert. 'Of course, I *did* have commitments . . . invitations I'd issued.' She perked up as she caught Noah's level stare. 'Oh, well, that can all be changed. Just family, honey. We're going to have an absolutely divinely mad time . . . in a quiet sort of way.'

I should have guessed from the vagueness of Marlaine's tone that she would find it impossible to keep her part of the bargain with Noah. I sensed a reluctance to cancel invitations she had already extended to heaven only knew how many of her jet set acquaintances, but that evening she was determined to maintain the compromise truce with her husband. *How* reluctant she was, and *how* impossible it was for Marlaine to separate herself from her social set, I was not to learn until moments before the chartered yacht departed from Port of Spain.

TEN

'Just family' from Marlaine's viewpoint could have included anyone she had known for more than six weeks. During the week before we embarked for Port-au-Prince, there were several bitter quarrels with Noah. There were tearful pleas, also, and a variety of justifications for adding to the guest list.

Irena Travalgnini was practically 'family,' Marlaine insisted. Besides, it would be disastrous to travel without the benefit of Countess Irena's astrological and psychic advice. The white-haired mystic's ex-husband, a mousy little man who for the past fourteen years had been writing a biography of some obscure Chaldean magician, appeared at the villa one morning, and Marlaine used romance and Noah's old-fashioned philosophy of marriage as an excuse to invite Count Giuseppe Travalgnini. 'After all these lonely years, destiny has brought these two soul mates together again, darling. The cruise will be like a second honeymoon for them. Isn't that *beautiful*, Noah?'

Noah gave in, anxious to keep harmony. Besides, there was only one month to go before he would have everything *his* way. He could afford to indulge Marlaine's whims for that long. She had, after all, made no fuss about his disposal of Wesley Reed.

By the time the gleaming white yacht left the island of Trinidad behind, bound for Port-au-Prince, our 'family' included not only the Travalgninis, but Yvette Girardoux (who would be no trouble at all because she was lost in a drugged world of her own and barely spoke to anyone); Bunny Stafford IV (who would leave us at some undetermined port of call where a tennis match was scheduled); Tish Vandercourt (who couldn't be separated from Bunny, and who needed the tranquillity of a cruise because her Texas oilman ex-husband was being an absolute swine about alimony payments); Ernesto Sandoval de Lopez de Sevilla (who would only go as far as Caracas, where he had business interests); and an American couple with the improbable names of Toby and Toni Fitzpaugh.

In their early thirties, the Fitzpaughs had inherited 'just oodles of money' upon the demise of an uncle who had invented and manufactured carnival rides. They were in the Caribbean to 'get away from the children for a while,' and apparently their offspring were terrors to be avoided, for the parents had been away from home for more than a year! Marlaine found the pair amusing ('The *nouveaux riches* are so divinely vulgar'), and although neither she, nor anyone else, determined which of the Fitzpaughs was Toby and which was Toni, she felt that a 'legitimate

115

married couple who've been together ten whole years' would add a 'wholesome touch, for Gee Gee's benefit.' Noah commented that he hoped the Fitzpaughs' three children were being raised by an equally wholesome governess, but he had given in on the matter of these two additions as he had to Marlaine's other invitations.

'It's only fair,' Noah said to me our first evening out to sea.

Marlaine was 'consulting' with Irena in the Travalgninis' cabin, and the rest of our party was also below deck, some, like Durwood, confined to their quarters by seasickness and the hardier guests playing bridge and drinking up a storm in the yacht's sumptuously fitted recreation salon.

I had left Gee Gee in the cabin we shared (though 'cabin' seems a crude way to describe a thickly carpeted, ultra-modern suite furnished by a world-famous interior decorator!), happily recording the day's events in one of the school composition books she used as her diary. She had filled reams of paper since our first meeting, keeping the journals locked in a suitcase which could hold nothing else. Looking forward to a breath of the balmy night air and a glimpse of the stars, I had found Noah enjoying the same benefits.

At his invitation, I had settled myself in a deck lounge next to the one Noah had chosen for himself, and after we had talked about the

116

loveliness of the night and the thrill of being on the open sea, we had drifted to the subject of Marlaine's guests.

'It's only fair,' he repeated. 'It would have been embarrassing for Marlaine to cancel invitations she'd made over a month ago. And the new people she's added . . .' He paused, probably trying to think of a reasonable excuse for their presence. 'My wife's an impulsive person and—I think you'll agree—a very kind person. Heaven knows, she isn't selfish. Frankly, I hadn't realized that this tub was one step down from an ocean liner.'

'Neither had I,' I admitted. 'I visualized a sailboat, with people falling all over each other on the deck.'

Noah laughed. 'I certainly didn't imagine two fireplaces and a projection room. It's a floating hotel. My point is, it would have been rather piggish to have most of the cabins unoccupied. Since Marlaine had already gone to the expense of a month's charter, I couldn't very well stop her from sharing the experience with people she's fond of.'

'It must be a kind of a delicate situation for you,' I ventured.

'Being married to a woman who can afford to spend more in one month than even the most fabulously successful doctor can earn in a year?' Noah sighed. 'It's a little rough for me to contemplate, yes. The thing is, Marlaine's always had money, so she takes it for granted.

Thinks nothing of it, except that she's very conscious of using it to make people happy. Sharing with . . .'

'With people who *need* help?' The criticism had slipped from me inadvertently. It was obvious that Marlaine's gifts, her parties, her support of house guests, were a luxury that pleased her, kept her surrounded by admiring friends, and served no altruistic purpose. With the exception of Wesley Reed and the Travalgninis, any of Marlaine's friends could have struggled along on their own millions. Determined that I would never make a comment implying that Noah's marriage was based on a shaky foundation, I tried to cover up my faux pas. 'I'm sure Marlaine contributes to dozens of worthy causes. She has every right to be generous with her friends.'

It was too dark to see Noah's face, but I was sure of a dubious expression, because the doubt crept into his voice. 'Yes, I expect she writes off contributions to charities.' He was eager to get away from the uncomfortable subject, sounding facetious as he said, 'It's too bad she can't write off all those cases of booze they brought aboard last night. Call it rubbing alcohol and take it off the income tax as a medical expense.'

Noah's reference to the liquor supply was also an unfortunate slip. He was reminded that he had been adamant about this being a dry cruise, embarrassed because now he felt obligated to explain to me why he had backed down. 'I couldn't ask Marlaine to be inhospitable,' he said. 'I'm not trying to force the pledge on the international set, after all. My only concern was with Marlaine.'

'And she's been doing beautifully,' I was able to observe. 'I think it's going to be a wonderful trip, Noah. Gee Gee's been incredible. Pleasant, cooperative. You were right about her. Now that she's convinced that someone actually cares about her, she's knocking herself out to be a model teen-ager.'

'I notice,' he said. 'The Fitzpaugh woman . . . what's her first name?'

'Toby or Toni.'

'Yes, Toby or Toni told me this afternoon that if her kids were half as well-mannered, she wouldn't have to get away from them to preserve her sanity.'

We exchanged idle comments about the people aboard, about the unobtrusive efficiency of the crew, the probable length of time it would take us to reach our first port of call. When we had tired of small talk, we discussed our experiences with patients, the problems of getting a medical education, our hopes for the future of our profession. Noah even talked about his father, and, in spite of that crotchety physician's current anger with his son, how pleased he would be to welcome him back to the fold.

I don't know how long we talked, but we

were relaxed together for the first time, our conversation rich with our common interests and aspirations. An occasional ripple of laughter came from below the deck. Apart from that, the soft purr of the yacht's twin engines and the lapping of water against her hull were the only sounds to compete with our voices. We talked quietly, impressed by an awesome sense of solitude.

I don't remember which one of us suddenly realized that it must be extremely late. 'I told Marlaine I'd wait for her up here,' Noah said, getting out of the canvas lounge chair abruptly. 'She can't still be cooped up with Irena. There's not *that* much to be seen in a crystal ball.'

I got up, too, hurrying along the port deck to keep up with Noah's nervous stride. He seemed guilt-racked at having neglected Marlaine for so long, although she was the one who had promised to meet him on deck. 'She must have forgotten,' Noah said vaguely.

'Maybe she fell asleep,' I suggested. 'This sea air really . . .'

A strident laugh echoed up the passageway as we started down the steps. There was no mistaking that shrill, hysteria-tinged laughter; Marlaine being the madcap hostess, Marlaine inviting everyone to live for the moment. Marlaine drinking.

Noah muttered a single 'Damn!' under his breath. He raced down the steep stairs, too

120

upset to notice whether I was accompanying him to the salon. He ran ahead of me, bursting into the room where Marlaine's friends had been playing bridge earlier. The door closed behind him while I hesitated in the narrow corridor outside. I didn't wait to hear the inevitable explosion. There would be angry words, an emotion-charged argument, tears, recriminations, promises, and, finally, kisses of forgiveness. I didn't want to be a witness to that exasperating scene again, or any part of it. I headed for my berth.

By the time I had got ready for bed, moving quietly because Gee Gee was asleep, the Haydens had taken their argument into the passageway. As Noah tried to get Marlaine into their master suite, her high-pitched cry of 'What are you trying to do . . . *destroy* me?' defied the yacht's soundproofing.

Then I heard Noah's voice, weary from having repeated the same words time and again: 'I'm trying to stop you from killing yourself, honey!' After that, with their door apparently closed, I heard nothing more.

I was grateful that Gee Gee hadn't been awakened. She had been responding so dramatically to the new 'family atmosphere' that I dreaded the thought of having her security shaken again. As I reached to click off the light by which Gee Gee had been writing before falling asleep, I breathed a silent prayer that by morning Noah and Marlaine would have their differences patched and Gee Gee would not know that her mother had been drinking or that there had been another rift.

I was a naive idiot. I had forgotten that Gee Gee made it her business to see everything, hear everything, know everything. As my fingers touched the lamp switch, Gee Gee opened her eyes wide. I was pinned by that unblinking reptilian stare for what seemed to be an endless span of time, though it lasted for only a second or two; that strangely inhuman yellow glinted gaze that bored through me like a laser beam and told me, *'Yes, I know M.E. is bombed again and Noah is furious with her. I also know that you and Noah have been enjoying yourselves together in that quiet, dark intimacy under the stars. I know you're in love with him and I know you're a moralistic cretin who aches with guilt for wanting Noah. I know, I know, I know all there is to know, including your horror at being stared at this way, because I know what YOU'RE thinking, Ferris Wheel. But you haven't the foggiest notion of what goes on in MY mind, do you? You don't know what I'm thinking, but it frightens you, doesn't it, Warden? And you see I'm amused. Cat and mouse. You, mousy; me, kitty. Purr-rr. Mee-yow. SCR-A-TCH!'*

Imagination? Tiredness? Guilt? I could have attributed that message to any of the three, though if there ever existed a case for thought transference, it could have been documented in that cabin on that night. I could have sworn that I actually *heard* Gee Gee's words. Yet there was nothing but that baleful, snickering, momentary impact of her eyes penetrating my mind.

It was over before my hand could turn the light switch, before I could express surprise at seeing Gee Gee awake. Only the shock of the dark-lashed hazel eyes open and staring, then closed again, locking a secret door which Durwood and Noah and I had foolishly thought we had entered, analyzing that incomprehensible dark region beyond.

Then my fingers moved and there was darkness. The yacht droned its steady course for Port-au-Prince. For miles around me, the sea was tranquil; above, glimpsed through a porthole, the constellations twinkled, eternally aloof, unthreatening. Why, then, did I lie awake, trembling, my heart pounding an erratic tattoo, the acrid taste of fear parching my mouth?

ELEVEN

An integral part of Gee Gee Sargent's genius was making you wonder, the next morning, why you had conjured up such ridiculous thoughts about her.

She was sweetness and light itself when she

123

joined me on the sun deck after breakfast. She was Rebecca of Sunnybrook Farm, Honeybunch at Sea, Sweet Genevieve on her very first cruise, and girlishly thrilled with the wonder of it all.

That mood, coupled with Marlaine's fervent pledge to stay sober and 'never, never again risk losing my lovely, lovely family,' made for an idyllic situation during the next two days. Irena beamed with a secretive smile; hadn't she *told* Marlaine that a minor negative incident should be ignored, because it would be followed by the most propitious signs imaginable?

I relaxed. I had fun. I played shuffleboard with Gee Gee and the Fitzpaughs. In the convivial atmosphere that pervaded, I found myself chatting easily with Bunny Stafford and Tish Vandercourt, listening to Count Travalgnini's problems with writing a book that 'publishers will never touch because it is not *commercial*; as though I, an artist, wished to lower myself to their crass level.' I was even able to go through the motions of at least *sounding* like a nurse when Yvette Girardoux engaged me in a conversation about barbiturates, although she obviously knew more about drugs, from firsthand experience, then I would ever learn from pharmacology texts.

I let the sun warm me, the sight of the crayon-blue sea satisfy my yearning for beauty.

People smiled, played games, sang songs, and danced under the stars at night. If it hadn't been for the ache created by my growing love for Noah Hayden, I could have said that I was having a glorious time.

There were two incidents during our stopover in Haiti that disturbed this pleasant state. First, there was Marlaine's receipt of a cablegram at Port-au-Prince. She divulged the contents to no one, not even Noah, and promptly slid into a deep depression that resisted all attempts to cheer her up.

Noah was too worried about her to enjoy the colorful atmosphere of the Haitian city, and he was crushed by Marlaine's refusal to communicate with him. 'I'm your *husband*,' I heard him reminding her. 'Honey, if something's wrong, I want to know about it. Help out . . . at least share the misery. What's wrong?'

'Nothing you'd be interested in,' Marlaine told him. 'And nothing you can do anything about. I'd like a drink, Noah. If you want to do something for me, don't give me a lecture, don't flutter around me like a mother hen. Just tell the steward to send over a Scotch on the rocks.'

Noah had no recourse. He stayed on board with Marlaine while everyone else went sightseeing ashore. Durwood and I took Gee Gee on a tour of the native market. We shopped rather halfheartedly, then ran into

125

the rest of our party at a restaurant where the plush decor and elaborate Creole cuisine offered a sharp contrast to the grinding poverty of the Haitian people, a pathetic condition that the dollar-hungry tourism bureau had attempted, unsuccessfully, to hide from view.

'You don't see many beggars,' Durwood told me. 'I understand the government rounded them up and whisked them off, up into the hills, to avoid depressing the tourists. I find that doubly depressing, myself.'

Gee Gee had barely touched her Shrimp Louie. 'I'm awfully low, myself.' In a voice that none of Marlaine's friends at the next table could help hearing, she added, 'I'm so worried about Mumsy. She looked so unhappy when we left.'

Durwood assured her that Noah would do his best to snap Marlaine out of her depression, but Gee Gee refused to be consoled. 'I just can't have a good time if my mother's miserable,' she insisted.

Durwood had promised her a taste of Haitian night life, but he agreed that Marlaine's unaccountable mood had affected him, too, and we went back to the yacht shortly afterward. Ironically, Gee Gee went straight to her diary, while Durwood reported that he was ready for 'a shower, a good book, and bed.' Neither of them looked in on or asked about Marlaine.

I found her sitting alone at the bar in the recreation salon, her green eyes glassy, her mood untypically dismal.

'Noah's gone up on deck to get some air,' she told me. 'Poor darling, he's worn himself out trying to get me out of this blue funk.' Marlaine patted the barstool next to hers. 'Perch, Roxy. I know better than to ask if you want a drink.'

'Thanks, but I've just finished a monstrous dinner.'

'Monstrous bad or monstrous big?' Marlaine forced a wan smile.

'Monstrous big.'

'You weren't gone long.'

'We were worried about you.'

The green eyes widened. 'You were? Really? How perfectly sweet of you. Durwood, too?'

'And Gee Gee,' I said.

For an instant, I thought Marlaine was going to cry. Then, leaning toward me so far that she nearly lost her balance, she whispered, 'For the record, darling . . . Gee Gee despises me.' I protested, but Marlaine gave me a long, wise look. 'Despises me,' she repeated.

There was a sullen pause, during which I tried to think of something cheerful to say. Marlaine broke the silence first. 'I'm terribly fortunate to have Noah,' she said.

I agreed.

'I wish I appreciated him. What's wrong

with me, Roxy? I keep searching, searching. Looking for . . . what? Whatever it is . . .' Marlaine refilled her glass from a pinch bottle on the bar, swallowed a mouthful, shuddered, and then said, 'Whatever it is, when I get wherever I think it's going to be . . . poof!' She made an uncoordinated attempt to snap her fingers. 'It's not there.'

'Maybe Noah's right,' I suggested. 'Stop looking. Stop running.'

Marlaine giggled, but the sound came out sounding like a dirge. ' 'S funny. That's what Noah keeps saying. "Stand still and let yourself be loved." That's so easy to say. Then you go on, year after year, yelling, "Eureka, I have found it! This is it!" And, time after time, you discover that this *isn't* it. When you've been disappointed so many times . . .'

'But you aren't going to be disappointed this time,' I said. 'Look, you're married to a man who isn't even remotely interested in . . . in fact, even resents . . . your money. He cares about *you*. Your health, your . . .'

'Noah's a beautiful person.' Marlaine held her glass up to eye level, swirling the contents and staring into the amber fluid. 'But he's a dreamer, Roxy. Dreamer and a martyr. All tied up with puritan conditioning that won't let him admit he's made a whopping big boo-boo. He's going to make this marriage stick if it kills him.' Marlaine imitated Noah's whistling sigh. 'And it's killing him. Frankly, I've never felt

128

sorry for any of my husbands. I feel terribly sorry for Noah.'

Marlaine made one more admission before Noah returned. Not an admission, really, but a hint at what was bothering her. Apropos of nothing, she looked directly at me and asked, 'It hasn't been too bad for you, being poor, has it, darling?'

I smiled and told her I'd never thought of myself as impoverished. 'I've always had everything I needed. I don't have to worry about having a job, and my income is enough to . . .'

'I guess you don't understand,' Marlaine said wearily. She was talking to herself more than to me when she added, 'I meant . . . not being able to do *anything* you want to do, whenever you want to do it. Wherever.' She made a shuddering motion, and I guessed at the message in that cablegram she had received. Noah would rejoice, I thought, at news that his wife was no longer the Kingsley heiress. But for Marlaine, even the threat of such a possibility from her father was too devastating to contemplate. It was clear to me, then, that Marlaine had no confidence in any of her attractions as a human being. Without money, unlimited amounts of money with which to buy friendship, adulation, love, she was convinced that she could not survive!

I got another inkling of the problems with which that poor little rich girl was saddled a few days later, when we cruised to Cap Haïtien. While we gazed up at the gloomy citadel atop a three-thousand-foot mountain, I noticed that Gee Gee had separated herself from the rest of the party and was staring up at that forbidding fortress with the most enraptured expression I had ever seen on any face. Walking over to join her, I noticed that Gee Gee was trembling, dots of perspiration forming on her temples. 'Kind of ... overwhelming, isn't it?' I suggested.

'It's fantastic,' Gee Gee breathed. 'It's so ... unbearably exciting!' She didn't turn that awed expression away from the ugly fortress. 'That Henri Christophe must have been a genius. Imagine getting three hundred and sixty cannon up that mountain.'

'It doesn't take genius to do something like that,' I said. 'Just total callousness. I've forgotten how many men died, building that citadel, Gee Gee, but I get sick just thinking about it. So much suffering, just because some power-mad emperor . . .'

'You miss the point,' Gee Gee said curtly. 'I suppose you're thinking it was all a waste. I mean, considering that the guns were supposed to protect the island from Napoleon. And he got busy elsewhere, so he never did attack.'

'Well, it was a terrible waste of lives,' I said.

'You don't appreciate the excitement of sheer genius formulating an impossible plan

130

. . . and then making it a reality.' I saw Gee Gee's eyes narrow, the faintly superior smile playing around her mouth. 'In a superior mind, the unthinkable becomes the inevitable. It's a fascinating process. I wouldn't expect you to understand.'

Later, viewing the Palace of Sans Souci, from which Emperor Christophe had conducted his bloody reign, Gee Gee experienced the same frightening emotional reaction. 'Can't you almost smell blood and hear wild shrieks?' she asked me.

I tried to dismiss her fascination with horror. 'Those so-called voodoo drums we're hearing are furnished by the Tourist Bureau, I imagine.'

She threw a contemptuous glance my way. 'You still moaning about those few crummy, expendable natives, Miss Ferris?'

I was thoroughly disgusted with her by then. Especially since she had made a point of telling everyone else in our party that she didn't want to go sightseeing this morning if there was going to be 'anything scary or bloody, like sacrificing roosters and stuff.' I returned the scathing look and snapped, 'No one's life is expendable!'

I was rewarded with a bemused smile that told me I was wrong. I avoided Gee Gee for the rest of our stay on Haiti. It was too unsettling to see an attractive sixteen-year-old girl so completely engrossed in a bloody, turbulent episode from the past, identifying completely with a ruthless 'genius.'

Avoiding Gee Gee and her admiration for 'an impossible plan' that had been realized, was a mistake for which I am not yet ready to forgive myself. I should have told the Haydens and Durwood what I had heard. But I was feeling sorry enough for Marlaine without telling her that her only child found bloodshed 'thrilling'?

It was a mistake. A terrible mistake for which I now assume full responsibility. Though I'm not sure anyone would have taken my warning seriously, especially since Gee Gee announced to everyone concerned that she hoped our next port of call, Kingston, Jamaica, would be 'less scary.' Wide-eyed, girlish, Sweet Genevieve won the sympathy of all with her loving statement: 'Mumsy's looking so sad as it is. Let's go to some *fun* place. I'd like to hear her laugh again, the way she used to.'

TWELVE

It was a nightmare about the citadel at Cap Haïtien that awoke me from my sleep. Our yacht had eased out to sea at four that afternoon, bound for Kingston. An unaccountable weariness had come over me shortly after dinner, and I had gone to bed early, falling asleep to the rhythmic scribbling of Gee Gee's ball-point pen.

I opened my eyes, shocked into awareness by the gruesome voodoo ritual that had invaded my dreams. I don't know what instinct prompted me to turn on the light above my berth or to look, immediately, toward Gee Gee's bed. Nor do I know why I *expected* to find her gone.

I got up quickly, noticing that the bathroom light was off and that the door was open; she was not in the cabin, then. My watch, which rested on a built-in dressing table, read 1:07. It was not as late as I thought, then; Gee Gee might have gone to join a party in the salon. There was no reason for alarm, yet I felt responsible for her. I tossed a robe over my pajamas and, barefoot, I padded out into the corridor.

There was no one in the salon and only night lights burned on the deck. I encountered one crew member, who told me that everyone had 'retired unusually early tonight, Miss.' He had not seen Miss Sargent. Neither had the second member of the night watch, to whom he called out the question.

Worried, after the crewman had helped me with a search of all except the private quarters on the yacht, I was relieved to find Durwood's cabin door slightly ajar. A timid knock brought him to the doorway, wide awake, explaining that he couldn't sleep and had been reading a new best-seller about the stock market.

'She's got to be *somewhere*,' Durwood said, after he and I had retraced the steps I had taken earlier. 'You're sure she's not in your cabin? The bathroom? In the shower?'

'I looked there.' If my own disturbed feeling was any indication, the fruitless search was too great a strain for Durwood. 'Maybe she's with her mother and Noah. I hate to disturb them, but there's no sense in your staying up half the night if Gee Gee's fallen asleep on their sofa. Why don't you go back to your book and let me . . .'

'I can't relax until we find the kid,' Durwood said irritably. He was with me when I knocked on the door to the Haydens' suite.

Groggy, Noah said, 'No, she's not here,' when I asked about Gee Gee. Then, realizing that he hadn't really checked, he said, 'Just a second . . . let me look.'

Noah returned to the door a few seconds later, wide awake now, his face drained of its color. 'Gee Gee's not here. Marlaine isn't, either!'

'They're somewhere talking,' Durwood concluded. But, like Noah and me, he seemed unconvinced.

There are just so many places where one can search aboard even a large yacht. At the end of a twenty-minute effort that became more frantic as even such unlikely places as the galley and the projection room were

134

searched, Noah roused the rest of the crew. We began a systematic search, then, of the cabins, the alarm increasing as we were joined by the awakened occupants.

Irena did nothing to help morale with her ominous revelation of having seen a 'mysterious black spot' in her crystal ball early that evening. Completely unnerved, Noah barked, 'Will you shut up, Irena?' He hurried off to help one of the sailors lift canvas shrouds from the lifeboats, a bizarre effort, and one not likely to yield results. But the only alternative, by that time, was to conclude that Gee Gee and her mother were nowhere aboard.

Irena was miffed, but it was she who found Gee Gee, sound asleep in her berth. I nearly fainted with relief. 'You see?' Irena gloated. 'You only *thought* the child was not in your cabin. I was led by unseen forces to look where no one else looked, yes? Now, let us go and find Marlaine in her bed, where that hysterical husband of hers plainly failed to see her.'

This time, Irena's 'unseen forces' failed her. Marlaine was not in the Haydens' suite. She was not in any of the places covered over and over again by the passengers and the crew. It was after four A.M. when the captain, an unsmiling British mariner of the old school, reached the reluctant conclusion that Mrs. Hayden was not anywhere aboard the yacht.

A dark pall settled over everyone involved

in the search as Noah cried out, 'But she's *got* to be here . . . somewhere!'

There were no more hiding places to be uncovered, yet for another hour or more all of us continued the search. Dawn had lighted the glassy sea before Noah, desperate and exhausted, sank into a deck chair, covered his face with his hands, and groaned, 'Oh, my God . . . Marlaine! Marlaine . . . why?'

'What are we going to tell that poor child?' Mrs. Fitzpaugh whispered to no one in particular.

We were gathered on the foredeck, helpless, incredulous, unable to believe what had become more obvious with every hour that passed: Marlaine had gone overboard. No one conjectured about whether her disappearance was the result of an accident (unlikely, with the sea so calm and the deck rails so high, yet, if she had been drinking . . .) or suicide. We were too numb to think, too stunned to do anything but exchange uneasy glances, with only an occasional comment uttered, then followed by a deadly silence:

'I can't believe it!'

'I *still* can't accept it.'

'That poor little girl!'

'I wouldn't have the heart to tell her.'

'The engine room! Did anyone think to . . .'

'We searched the engine room, ma'am. I'm very sorry.'

I remember it now like a surrealistic dream;

it was assumed Marlaine had been drinking and that she had fallen overboard by accident. There was only one discreet question about whether Mrs. Hayden had been 'despondent.'

Oddly, it was Durwood who supplied a defensive answer. 'I don't know who told you that, sir. My cousin had been somewhat depressed, but it was over a . . . trivial matter. She had her moods, as we all do, but she always bounced back quickly. There's no question of . . .' Durwood glanced at Gee Gee and avoided the indelicate suggestion of suicide, letting the inspector supply the missing word. 'Mrs. Hayden was an extremely cheerful, gregarious . . .'

'*She was miserable!*' Gee Gee's cry stabbed through the room like a lightning bolt. 'She knew Miss Ferris was trying to take Noah away from her!'

Durwood's face turned scarlet and Noah sat upright, scowling.

'The child's upset . . .' Durwood started to explain.

Gee Gee was not to be silenced. I caught my breath as she stood up, pointing her finger at me. 'Why do you think she told everybody I was out of my room last night? Somebody saw *her* out on the deck, that's why! She had to make up an excuse . . . say she was looking for me.'

'I was looking for you!' I cried.

'Everybody knows I was in my bed.' Gee

Gee blotted at her tear-swollen eyes. 'Countess Irena . . . *you* know.'

I saw Irena's head bob in solemn agreement. Unbelieving, I was suddenly the focus of attention from Marlaine's friends, as Gee Gee sobbed out an intricate drama that cast me in the role of a passion-driven schemer, determined to win Noah Hayden for myself after having 'used poor Uncle Durwood and then broken his heart.' Immobilized by shock, I heard Gee Gee accuse me of trying to undermine her love for her mother, of trying to seduce Noah during clandestine walks on the beach, and a late rendezvous on the deck. Ingeniously, as though the plot had been painstakingly constructed by a superb novelist, Gee Gee recalled incidents that had been observed by the present witnesses, statements I had made before the others, taking them out of context and twisting them to suit her story. 'Oh, she looks sweet and innocent.' Gee Gee's anguished voice sounded so convincing that I was certain that she believed, at least at the moment, exactly what she was saying. 'But I know her. She wanted to get rid of my Mumsy. She couldn't get Noah any other way, *so she followed her up on deck last night and pushed her overboard.'*

'Gee Gee, that's not true!' Noah was on his feet, shaking with outrage. 'I know you've had a terrible shock, but you can't accuse someone of murder, just because . . .'

'You don't know,' Gee Gee wailed. She fell against Noah, choking on dry sobs, forcing him to place his arms around her.

'If you *please?*' Irena said indignantly. She addressed the elderly official, 'Can you not see that the child is in a state of collapse? With your permission, I will take the poor little girl to my quarters.'

Permission was granted, of course; Gee Gee had the sympathy of the investigators as well as that of the Countess, her ex-husband, the Fitzpaughs, Ernesto, Tish, Bunny, and Yvette. I felt like the accused at a medieval witchcraft trial, seeing the chill on the faces around me, noting with horror that even Durwood was eyeing me with an alien expression.

Only Noah refused to take the vicious accusation seriously. And it was his defense of me that tightened the noose. Listening to him argue that I was completely innocent of Gee Gee's vicious charges, I realized that he was not only convincing the others of my guilt, but implicating himself.

Exasperatingly, the inspector and his assistants, one of whom was taking down every statement in rapid shorthand, made no comment. He listened intently, more alert now that he seemed to be probing more than an accident. His silence encouraged others to join the fray.

Prompted by Gee Gee's cues, Marlaine's friends began to volunteer their own impressions. Tish Vandercourt recalled, 'I never did believe that Miss Ferris didn't want to take this cruise. She *pretended* that she didn't want to, and poor Marlaine naively encouraged her to come along. But it was *Mr.* Hayden who insisted.'

'A few nights ago,' Bunny Stafford remembered, 'I heard Marlaine screaming that her husband was trying to kill her.'

'*Destroy*,' Noah shouted. 'She used the word 'destroy,' not 'kill.' Marlaine was angry because I'd taken her away from the bar. She was referring to her social life, not to . . .'

'There were other incidents of this nature?' The snowy-haired inspector had broken his silence to address anyone who cared to supply an answer.

There was a barrage of replies:

'They were constantly quarreling.'

'Marlaine never had a moment's peace. He hounded her continually, finding fault, making public scenes, embarrassing her before guests.'

'Wesley Reed knew what was going on behind poor Marlaine's back. No wonder they managed to get rid of him!'

'He tried to stop her from killing herself with liquor!' I had cried out my defense of Noah before I realized that this was all Marlaine's staunch friends needed. Of course! Of course; a man resenting his impulsive marriage to an alcoholic wife, meeting a younger woman, the two of them plotting a

142

way to rid themselves of the heiress without losing her inheritance.

No one said the words, but they were implied in every glance; the atmosphere was thick with indictment. Durwood hadn't added fuel to the pyre, but his very silence was a form of accusation. 'It's not true!' I protested. 'All of it . . . the bits and pieces . . . it's all planned to make, it seem as though . . .'

'A *plan?*' The inspector's bushy white brows were raised slightly. His voice remained calm and softly modulated, yet I detected an iciness that hadn't been present before. 'Who would make such a plan, Miss . . . ah . . . Miss Ferris? And for what conceivable reason?'

'I don't know her reason!' Tears threatened to overwhelm me and I made an effort to control myself. 'I don't know why Gee Gee would want to accuse me of murder. I only know . . .'

Where to begin? With my first conversation with Marlaine's precocious daughter, in which Gee Gee had revealed that she hated 'M.E.,' and was attracted to her new stepfather? With a recital of the many times the cobra eyes had revealed their amusement when Noah and Marlaine had quarreled? With a description of Gee Gee's intense excitement while viewing the citadel at Cap Haïtien, a repetition of her words? What had she said? Something about an impossible plan becoming an inevitability when formed in the mind of a genius.

Something about people being 'expendable.'

I tried to convey what I knew about Gee Gee Sargent. I failed miserably. She had presented concrete statements, specific incidents, witnesses. I was offering disjointed impressions, conjectures, placing words in Gee Gee's mouth, phrases so shocking that her carefully conditioned sympathizers gasped at my audacity.

'Inspector, this is . . . this is virtually *blasphemous!*' I knew how completely I had failed, because that was Durwood Kingsley objecting. 'My niece may be emotionally disturbed, but anyone who's been around her knows that she adores . . . adored her mother. I can't imagine Miss Ferris saying such defamatory things about a grieving child!'

'Trying to shift the blame!' a female voice screeched out.

They were all talking at once, then, with the inspector attempting to quiet them without raising his voice, repeating, 'Ladies and gentlemen . . . ladies and gentlemen' in a monotonous drone that emphasized the unreality of the scene. It was as dreamlike as Alice's mock trial in Wonderland, with only Noah refraining from the chorus of cries demanding my head. He stood next to his chair, agonized and bewildered, looking like a man wanting to run but not knowing where.

We were dismissed by the Jamaican authorities, but cautioned that private

144

interviews would be wanted. Furthermore, upon docking at Kingston, no one was to leave the yacht without permission. No mention was made of murder, or even of suspected foul play. But Gee Gee, for whatever reason she had in mind, had succeeded in making me a suspect.

Marlaine's friends remained in the salon, no doubt to console themselves with the Scotch their hostess had considerately left behind, and to dredge up recollections that would further incriminate Noah and me.

Durwood, shaken by the proceedings, and apparently too embarrassed to face me, hurried out of the room. Noah and I were left with the uncomfortable choice of ignoring each other, which would have appeared an obvious attempt to disassociate ourselves because of guilt, or to walk out together, giving our judges more ammunition. Fortunately, we were spared the decision when the inspector, or whatever he was, asked if he might have a conference with Mr. Hayden on deck. I left the salon alone, sensing the hate-filled stares that followed me, feeling like a culprit.

It was inconceivable, yet it was really happening. Alone in the cabin I had shared with Gee Gee (Irena had made it clear that the girl would be 'safer' in her quarters) I tried to release the unbearable pressure with tears, but tears refused to come.

I had to live with the nightmare, then,

though tension threatened my sanity. Marlaine was dead; how she had died was a mystery. Yet a convincing case had been built, pointing at me as the murderess! *Why?*

Out of this ghastly question, there arose another, and this one flooded me with horror. Gee Gee's lies, her efforts to establish herself as an adoring daughter, the cat-and-mouse game she played with me, were all units in a meticulously thought out plan. It was beyond my comprehension, but there was no doubting it now; Gee Gee had started engineering this situation from the moment she had met Noah, choosing me as the logical patsy in a plot to rid herself of a mother she detested.

No, it was too shocking. A sixteen-year-old girl didn't decide she wanted her handsome stepfather for herself, along with her mother's inheritance. A child wouldn't push her mother into the sea and then accuse an innocent person of that heinous crime. It couldn't be, it *couldn't*, my mind insisted. Even if Gee Gee were capable of this monstrous evil, would she have hinted as much to me? She could as easily have deceived me as she had the others, convincing me with her superb acting that she worshiped her lovely 'Mumsy.'

I remembered, then, Gee Gee's perverse delight in letting me know that she was infinitely more clever than I. Letting me know what she was doing had added a fillip to her ugly game. I represented competition, I had to be eliminated. But how tempting to the ego of a self-styled genius to let the victim know she was being victimized!

I paced the cabin, trying to delve into the tortuous chambers of (I was convinced of it now) a pathologically evil brain. It was too much for me, and I could turn to no one for comfort. Durwood had swallowed Gee Gee's line whole. Noah could not dare to be seen talking to me alone. I would be shunned by everyone else on board.

For a long time; I gazed out through the porthole, seeing the blinking lights of Kingston grow brighter as the yacht sped toward its destination. Then, seized by a sudden fury at the injustice of my position, I stomped over to the suitcase in which Gee Gee kept her voluminous diaries. Surely there would be something written there that would exonerate me. Gee Gee wouldn't have been able to resist recording her day-to-day triumphs; she would gloat about it, perhaps even detail her intentions.

My hands shook as I lifted the two side latches, remembering in frustration that the suitcase was locked and that Gee Gee wore the tiny key suspended from a fine chain around her neck. Surprisingly, the lock snapped open at my touch; the suitcase was unlocked. Trembling as much outwardly as I was shaking inside, I opened the case and removed the current journal, which Gee Gee invariably placed on top of her other notebooks when she finished her nightly stint. I flipped the looseleaf notebook open at random, finding an entry that had been written during our stay in Port-au-Prince. My eyes were attracted to my own name and I read:

Roxy Ferris is so thoughtful and pleasant that I'll bet she's a fabulous nurse. I hope she decides to marry Uncle Durwood because I'd really dig to have her in our family.

It made no sense. Neither did the other innocuous entries that I scanned:

Mumsy's a living doll. Tonight she let me stay up late so that I could watch my very favorite Humphrey Bogart movie. When we go to live in Los Angeles I'll probably get to go to movie studios, and everything. Everything's so neat, lately. It's like a dream come true.

Another entry listed, in typical teen-age style, Gee Gee's favorite recording stars in order of preference. It was an ironic effort, since Gee Gee never listened to records and had no interest in popular music.

It dawned on me, then, adding to my fear, that the diary was not a record of Gee Gee Sargent's innermost thoughts. It was a public document, cleverly written to simulate the trivial jottings of an average, normal adolescent girl! Either I was completely mad, or Gee Gee was the most thorough, most diabolically clever sixteen-year-old liar who had ever drawn a breath. She had painted a more convincing portrait in writing than she had with words and actions. No one reading her 'diary' would have believed anything I had to say about Sweet Genevieve.

And, matching her brilliance, was my bumbling stupidity. I hadn't thought to lock the door before I began snooping. I was reading an entry that described the Cap Haïtien citadel in exactly the opposite terms from those Gee Gee had expressed, privately, to me, when I heard the latch turn.

Startled, I threw the notebook back into the suitcase, but it was too late. I was caught red-handed as Gee Gee stepped into the room, followed at a discreet distance by her uncle.

'Oh, look! Look what she's doing now!' Gee Gee cried. Her tone was piteous as she hurried forward to rescue her precious suitcase.

Durwood scowled as he crossed the cabin to help her.

'Now do you . . . see why I was afraid to come in alone?' Gee Gee wept. 'If I'd caught her alone . . .'

I started for the door, sick with humiliation, but furious, too. 'So now she's not only convinced you that I'm a murderess . . . I'm a danger to her, too!'

Durwood looked sheepish, avoiding my eyes. 'I just thought . . . I'd help Gee Gee pack her things. She . . . you know she's terribly disturbed, Roxy, and . . .'

'She's *psychotic!*' I cried. 'Are you so dense

that you don't . .'

Gee Gee had thrown herself over her suitcase, sobbing, 'Don't let her torture me anymore, Uncle Dur. Oh, please, please . . .'

'I'm sorry.' Durwood looked utterly confused and helpless. 'I'm sorry, Roxy, but this whole situation is . . .'

'Too much for you?' I asked. 'You saw what she did to the room at the villa. You couldn't control her then. What do you think she's . . .'

'For God's sake, have some compassion!' Durwood exploded. 'The child's lost her *mother!*'

'And she's accused me of murder,' I reminded him. 'What are you sorry about, Durwood? Sorry you got me into this mess? Or sorry that I'm a murderess? You believe her, don't you? You don't want to, but you actually believe I . . .'

'Please!' he muttered. He made an awkward attempt to get Gee Gee to her feet. His face looked blanched and I had a momentary fear that his heart would give out.

'I'll get out of the way and let you pack,' I said. My own legs were so shaky that I wasn't sure I could get to the door.'

Durwood had helped Gee Gee up from the floor and was saying something about letting one of the stewards do the packing, with perhaps Irena or Mrs. Fitzpaugh to supervise. 'You aren't up to this now,' I heard him say. Gee Gee responded with a thin, minor-keyed sound, like that of a wild forest creature gripped by excruciating pain.

The strangely inhuman sound alarmed me, my nursing sense reminding me that the most vicious psychotic was capable of intense suffering. What if Gee Gee was paranoic and actually believed that I had murdered her mother and was now a threat to her? Her torment would be unimaginable. I was not a judge. I was a *nurse,* a nurse who had been told that the girl suffered from some obscure 'nervous complaint.' I looked back, arrested by that pitiful cry. Durwood's back was turned toward me. Gee Gee was clinging to him (for comfort or for protection?), the top of her head just visible over his bent shoulder.

There was no letting up of that tortured sound, yet as my eyes locked with Gee Gee's, I saw that they were dry. *Dry, and shining with a delight that sent an icy shudder through my body!*

I had to clutch at a handrail near the door to keep from collapsing, knowing that Marlaine Kingsley Hayden's child was more than insane. For in that brief instant when our eyes met, Gee Gee *winked* at me. It was a slow, deliberate, knowing wink barbarously cruel. It was the triumphant communication of a demon straight out of hell!

FOURTEEN

'I don't know what Durwood wants,' Noah said. I had met him in the corridor near Durwood Kingsley's cabin, to which he, too, had evidently been summoned that morning. 'All I know is that he asked to see me here at ten-thirty.'

'I got the same message from the steward,' I told Noah.

We had reached Durwood's door, and Noah raised his hand to knock, then hesitated. He looked exhausted from lack of sleep, his face set in grim lines, but there was a heart-warming tenderness in his eyes. I knew the harassment he had been undergoing, both from the police and from the other passengers, who were furious at being detained aboard the yacht, and pressing for an arrest. I yearned to take Noah in my arms, to assure him that he was not alone. In that moment before he knocked on the door, a long, meaningful look told me that Noah understood my misery, too, and longed to give me comfort. The kindest thing he could do, he seemed to be saying, was to avoid me. But he sympathized with my ordeal. He believed, completely, in my innocence and knew that I had faith in his.

There was only time for that brief exchange of reassurances before we were inside the cabin and Durwood was inviting us to sit down and apologizing, 'I didn't mean to send you two an officious summons. The problem is, I thought we ought to have a private talk, and the damned boat's swarming with investigators. Reporters, too, I suspect.'

Durwood was being extremely affable, but Noah remained politely cool. 'You asked to see us, Durwood. Why?'

Durwood's uneasiness was pitiful. 'Well, I .. . first of all, I wanted to assure both of you that I . . . in my testimony this morning, I made it abundantly clear that I attribute my niece's charges to her . . . severe emotional upset.'

'I lost my wife,' Noah said. 'That didn't give me the right to accuse someone else of . . .'

'No, no, of course not. But we all know Gee Gee's terribly disturbed. She can't be held responsible for what she says while she's in shock. The point I wanted to make was that I don't take her charges seriously, even though I . . . considering some of the circumstances . . . the fact that we were all too stunned to think clearly . . .'

'You've exonerated us,' Noah said. 'Thank you. May we go now, Durwood?'

'Come on, now, Noah. I've apologized.' Durwood made a gesture of helplessness. 'I'd also like to tell you I'm sorry that I tried to steer the police away from a suicide theory. I was trying to protect Gee Gee. I . . . thought it would be less painful to her if she assumed

153

Marlaine fell overboard accidentally.'

Noah raised his brows quizzically. 'You don't think she did?'

'Look, this is no reflection on you," Durwood insisted. 'I didn't want this to get out, but my cousin attempted suicide on at least half a dozen occasions that I know of. I managed to cover it up every time. Kept it from everyone except . . . the husband she appeared to be married to at the time.'

Noah winced. 'I didn't flatter myself that I'd be able to make Marlaine happy.'

'In any case, you weren't responsible for her despondency this time,' Durwood went on. 'I phoned my uncle, and I found out what he'd said to her in that cablegram that depressed Marlaine so terribly. He'd gotten word about that . . . unfortunate incident with Wesley Reed . . . Saw it in the papers, I imagine. He's divided his money between a trust fund for Gee Gee and a religious institution of some kind. As of the first of next month, Marlaine wasn't even going to receive her . . . rather generous allowance.'

'She hinted as much to me,' I said.

'So, you see, I've had no recourse but to let the police know the truth. You weren't responsible, either of you. I've reported my cousin's history of suicide attempts. And this new motive, which must have been a shattering blow to Marlaine.'

Noah looked over at me, his expression

154

stoic. 'Roxy shares my gratitude, I'm sure. Is that all?'

Durwood's face flushed, but he was eager to keep us in the cabin. 'Not really. I . . . understand your annoyance, but I also wanted you to see why I found it so aggravating to hear my niece painted as some sort of . . . matricidal monster.'

Before I could tell him about my latest encounter with Gee Gee, Durwood reached into a dresser drawer to extract several of the looseleaf notebooks I recognized as Gee Gee's diaries. 'I didn't like doing this . . . going through my niece's private papers. But I think they'll serve to convince you that you've been wrong, Roxy. The poor kid's as naive and enthusiastic and affectionate as any girl her age. If you'll read this, you'll see why I was so infuriated by your attempt to . . . well, you'll admit that nonsense about her penchant for human sacrifices and evil genius was grossly unfair.'

Durwood waved his pipe in an impatient gesture as I tried to interrupt him. 'Listen to this, people.' He sat down on a slat bench next to Noah, opening one of the notebooks in his lap. 'Tell me if this youngster hasn't been completely misunderstood. And then we'll clear the atmosphere . . . stop accusing each other of . . .'

'I've already read some of it,' I protested from my chair on the opposite side of the cabin. 'You don't understand! It's a brilliant piece of fiction!'

'Fiction!' Durwood glared at me. 'Roxy, I'm trying to be just. But if you persist in this . . . witchhunt of yours, I'm going to change my mind again. Noah, listen to this! The child's comments about Roxy. Her fondness for . . .'

'Wait a minute!'

Durwood's hand jerked at the sharp command from Noah. He had been turning the leaves of the notebook before him, the inevitable pipe in his right hand, too disturbed to notice that the lighted tobacco rested against the paper. Now, as Noah reached over to turn back one of the pages, Durwood made a startled sound. 'What's wrong?'

'The back of the sheet,' Noah pointed out: I got up, crossing the room to see what he was looking at so intently. 'There seems to be writing of some sort.'

It took only a few seconds' examination to show us that Gee Gee's diary, scrawled on only one side of each sheet of paper, was incomplete. By exposing the blank pages to the heat from Durwood's pipe, we produced patches of what appeared to be an equal amount of writing.

'Vinegar,' Noah said. 'It could be a patented secret ink of some kind, or just plain vinegar. I imagine if it were held up over a strong light bulb . . .'

'I don't like this,' Durwood objected. 'It's

prying into the girl's most personal ...'

'You were ready to go back to accepting Gee Gee's accusations against Roxy just a few seconds ago,' Noah said sharply. 'You were willing to pry into a diary that Roxy calls a fake, weren't you, Durwood? To prove your point. Well, I, for one, think there's too much at stake to worry about Gee Gee's sensibilities. I'm curious to know why she should keep two sets of records when she didn't have to worry about anyone reading the original.'

Durwood was visibly upset, but he was in no position to argue. Furthermore, although he was deeply disturbed, by what exposure to an unshaded light bulb brought forth on the first page, he was now drawn by the same compelling curiosity that had seized Noah and me.

It would have taken days, even weeks, to turn the seemingly blank pages into sheets covered with burnt brown inscriptions. But within the next hour, we had produced a sickening document that left all of us shaking and incredulous.

We read early entries, written while Gee Gee was enrolled at Shadowbrook School for Girls. They were a gloating record of intrigues and lies and character assassinations, ingeniously planned and executed without the least vestige of conscience. Even the brittle, calloused style of writing was eons removed from the girlish expressions written on the other side of the page:

'I used a double flanking motion today, wiring M.E. that my P.E. teacher is inordinately fond of me, which naturally sent Green Eyes into a tizzy. Not that she cares a rap about my morals (!), but how would it sound to Old Moneybags if he learned she was keeping her little darling in a den of corruption? I killed two birds with the proverbial you-know-what, because M.E. is considering springing me from this pest hole, and I hear via the grapevine that Miss Pearson, late of the Shadowbrook faculty, is getting the old heave-ho. Sometimes my brilliance astounds even me. Delicious irony: Pearson not only doesn't feel unwholesomely cozy toward me, she hates my guts. Ah, revenge. How sweet it is!'

There was another paragraph, written several days later, which Durwood read aloud with a horror-strained voice:

'No one doubts for an instant that Sneaky Sal broke her cranium in a fall from her horse. Delicious. Not the faintest association with her reporting me to the Head Jailer for that little tete-a-tete with the gardener. Her expression when I told her what I intended to do was memorable. A risky procedure on my part, but my timing was superb, as always, and I found dear Sally's reaction exhilarating, to say the least. An astute shrink would probably have a ball figuring out why I tingle at the sight of terror. Must remember to weep copious tears at chapel services tomorrow.'

158

'I can't believe this,' Durwood kept croaking. '*This* has got to be fiction. It's a . . . a short story of some kind. An assignment. I'm sure we'll find it's a school composition.'

Noah was less certain. Nor was there any further question when we reached the entries dated from Gee Gee's arrival in Trinidad. I think Noah had all he could do to keep nausea down as he read:

This entire safari has ostensibly been planned to "bring me closer" to my new daddy. Priceless, considering that I'm having all I can do to control the baser biological urges when Noah's around. Patience, patience. I'll have to play it cool. But what an inspiration I had today!

My original object was to keep dear Gramps informed (subtly, of course) of M.E.'s activities. Alas, the way she's going with that Wesley Reed creep, Old Moneybags is liable to cancel me along with her and make some absurd missionary school disgustingly rich. Too risky to contemplate. Logical alternative is to dispose of M.E. There will be a yummy bonus if only I can constrain myself from letting people know how intensely I loathe her and how fascinating I find Number Five.

Aghast, realizing that we were reading a blueprint for murder, we followed the development of Gee Gee's plan. It was like peering inside a coldly corrupt mind, and I could almost see Gee Gee propped up in her bed, her strange eyes glancing at me with amusement as she wrote:

'Apparently the cruise is definite. Providential break. What better place than at sea, among properly conditioned witnesses, where the details can become sufficiently garbled before the gendarmes are available.

'Yes, dear diary, I have decided against the Drunken Heiress Falls Overboard theory. Why not dispose of two competitors for Noah's affections in one fell swoop? I've been playing this angle, just in case. The Ferris Wheel has been conditioned to feel sorry for Number Five, trapped as he is, and it has been a simple matter to let everyone know that she is mad for Noah and violently resentful of M.E. A pity, actually, since Roxy's naivete amuses me. She is, however, as expendable as Sneaky Sal.'

There was a final notation, written shortly after our arrival in Port-au-Prince:

'It appears that my cable to Old Moneybags was effective. M.E. got the ax yesterday. I will have to apply my genius to convincing the old goat that my widowed stepdaddy is a fine moral specimen, to avoid being whisked off to Living Death at the Kingsley estate. Perhaps a line or two about Noah enrolling me in a Bible study class. However, this is a problem my superior mind will cope with later. In the meantime, I am faced with being deprived of seeing my master plan brought to flower. Green Eyes is despondent, tralala. Getting loaded in spite of Number Five's efforts and sulking about the loss

160

of all that lovely swag. I waited until the Ferris Wheel konked out last night and trailed M.E. on her tottering stroll around the deck. Methinks she drinketh with purpose now and looketh over the rail with unquestionable longing.'

There were no more entries in Gee Gee Sargent's secret journal. She had been too busy 'remembering to weep copious tears' to devote time to her precious diary.

Noah's hand was trembling as though he was suffering a malarial chill as he closed the notebook. Durwood had dropped to the edge of his bed and was staring into space. Noah and I exchanged professional glances; this was a recent cardiac patient. He had just been subjected to a devastating shock.

'You may be right,' Noah lied, his voice straining at calmness. 'This is probably an exercise in imagination, Durwood. Let's not get too upset until we're sure of our facts.'

Durwood shook his head back and forth slowly, undeceived. He was still sitting there when I returned with a sedative Noah prescribed for him before taking the private journals of Genevieve to the white-haired official in charge of the investigation.

FIFTEEN

I have only fragmentary memories of the maniacal scene in which Gee Gee was confronted with the evidence in her own handwriting.

Her shrieks, which filled the main salon and reverberated from every corner of the yacht, were those of a trapped animal. I was grateful that sedation had rendered Durwood Kingsley unconscious. Fortunately, he was spared the terrifying *coup de grace* of hearing his niece turn on Noah with a barrage of obscenities. Her rage, as two of the investigators restrained her by force, resembled that of a mad dog. And, perhaps predictably, she was less furious about exposure, with its probable consequences, than with the blow to her ego. Her 'superior mind' had been outwitted. The genius had made a mistake. She had destroyed any possibility of 'success,' and having irretrievably 'lost' Noah, she directed her screaming invectives at *him*.

Only later, when she had exhausted herself, and Durwood, awakened but still in a state of shock, insisted upon accompanying the authorities who took Gee Gee into custody, only then did she revert to her cool, sophisticated, brilliant image of herself.

Most of the crew and the guests were

gathered around in stunned semi-circle as Gee Gee was escorted from the yacht. A Jamaican government launch waited alongside. Shuffling disconsolately behind his niece, Durwood was bathed in horror once more as Gee Gee turned to fix him with one of her taunting stares. She was amused again, the goddess playing her game with lesser subjects once more, as she said, 'Please don't be so gloomy, Uncle Dur. I didn't do her in, honestly, luv.'

He choked on an unintelligible word and Gee Gee giggled at his agony. 'It would have been an exciting entry for my diary, but Mumsy was always depriving me of my fun. She did a do-it-yourself thing.' Every-one who was listening in awe-struck silence was included in Gee Gee's final remarks. Her dark bangs lifted from her forehead in the gentle breeze and she smoothed them down with her free hand. The other wrist was manacled to that of a plainclothesman. 'I didn't even get to see the grand exit, after following her around for a full hour. No help from me. All by herself. Y' know? *Sp-a-lash!*'

I have never experienced a more shuddering moment, nor do I expect to again. The rest of my stay aboard the yacht, and even the time spent in a Kingston resort hotel, while authorities gathered what they needed in the way of testimony, is blurred in my memory.

I do remember Noah's efforts, and my own,

163

to convince Durwood Kingsley that his confused sense of 'family responsibility' would serve no purpose and would further jeopardize his health. When he was finally assured that Noah would take over the responsibility for Gee Gee's commitment to a mental institution, Durwood appeared relieved. He had lived through a nightmare and now he was eager to escape the scene and shut it out of his mind.

He looked wan, as though he were drained out, when he came to my room to say goodbye and to apologize for not waiting for me. I was due for one more investigative session, with a court reporter to take down my statements about the conversations I had had with Gee Gee; my plane reservation had been made for the next day.

'I should really go back with you,' Durwood said. He shifted his pipe uneasily from one hand to the other. 'I got you into this predicament. The least I can do . . .'

'The best thing you can do is go back to the peace and quiet of your apartment,' I told him. 'Try to get back to normal as soon as possible. I'll manage, don't worry.'

'Yes, I suppose . . . with Noah looking after everything.' There was only the faintest hint of jealousy in Durwood's tone to remind me that this venture had started out as an attempt to sell me on the idea of marriage. Durwood had not only given up the idea, he was anxious to avoid the subject. Yet he must have felt that he owed me some sort of explanation. And he was further embarrassed, remembering that for a while he had been willing to accept the word of a psychotic relative when she accused me of murder.

'I don't know how to tell you how I feel, Roxy,' he began.

I rescued him from his predicament, asking abruptly, 'What are your plans? Going back to the old ticker tape, I expect. Stocks and bonds. The Dow Jones averages.'

His eyes avoided mine, but Durwood smiled vaguely. 'I'm a better judge of portfolios than people,' he conceded. Before we shook hands, after I had recited the usual trite precautions about taking care of his health, Durwood Kingsley walked out of my life with a justification for his interest in the stock market, and his decision to remain a bachelor: 'When you don't involve yourself in anything more personal than the stock market, the most you can lose is money.'

I said goodbye to someone else the next afternoon. Noah was apologetic, too, for not seeing me to the airport. But he didn't have to explain why it would have been ill-advised. When he reached out for my hand, as we waited for a porter to carry the luggage from my hotel room, Noah said quietly, 'I'm not going to say goodbye, Roxy. I hope you don't, either.'

I looked up into his eyes, seeing there the pain and sorrow that I had observed in our first meeting, but recognizing, too, a flicker of hope for the future. His ordeal was far from over. He had made a foolish mistake, but he was committed to paying the full price for it, although he was legally free from any responsibility for Gee Gee.

There were unpleasant matters to take care of; he was staying until they were settled, or until Gee Gee's grandfather provided attorneys to take charge. Or until the girl's real father was summoned.

There was a period of mourning and of rebuilding his own life before Noah, too. He was not truly free. Not yet, his eyes told me. But the day would come. The magnetism that had drawn me to him was not a one-way force. It was there, between us, potent and compelling. *Not now.* I read this wordless communication and understood. *Not now. Someday. Perhaps soon.*

Our fingers twined around each other for a lingering moment and I blinked back my tears. There would be an interval during which each of us might reflect on the tragic circumstances that had brought us together. Time to wonder whether a star-crossed woman who had searched for, and never found, happiness had been the cause of, or the victim of, the incredibly twisted personality of her only child. There would be time to reaffirm our respect for marriage and the solemn responsibility it entails. Time to reaffirm the importance of solid values, of selflessness, and, most important, of love.

'I won't say goodbye, Noah.' It was a whispered promise, and then Noah had let go of my hand and was gone.

Nearly a year has gone by since my ill-fated 'employment' as a jet set nurse. Yesterday, while I was nearing the end of this record (which, unlike Gee Gee's diary, has been set down for therapeutic purposes in an effort to cleanse a traumatic experience out of my system), a messenger brought a box of Talisman roses to my door. Grateful patients, once they're dismissed from the hospital where I now work as a general duty nurse, sometimes send flowers to express their appreciation. I glanced at the accompanying card casually.

It was not written in Noah's handwriting, of course; the roses had been ordered in Pasadena, California, and delivered by a florist in Brooklyn, where I now live. But the message, even if it had not borne Noah's name at the bottom, could only have come from him. It read:

'I still don't want to say goodbye. Arriving in New York and will call you Thursday morning to say hello. And much, much more. Love, Noah.'

This is Thursday morning. I've called my supervisor to request the day off. And now

there is nothing to do except try to keep from
exploding with joy while I wait for the phone
to ring.

We hope you have enjoyed this Large Print book. Other Chivers Press or Thorndike Press Large Print books are available at your library or directly from the publishers.

For more information about current and forthcoming titles, please call or write, without obligation, to:

Chivers Large Print
published by BBC Audiobooks Ltd
St James House, The Square
Lower Bristol Road
Bath BA2 3BH
UK
email: bbcaudiobooks@bbc.co.uk
www.bbcaudiobooks.co.uk

OR

Thorndike Press
295 Kennedy Memorial Drive
Waterville
Maine 04901
USA
www.gale.com/thorndike
www.gale.com/wheeler

All our Large Print titles are designed for easy reading, and all our books are made to last.